ON
SORROW

Raegan Teller

Pondhawk Press LLC
Columbia, South Carolina

Pondhawk Press LLC
PO Box 290033
Columbia, SC 29229

ISBN 979-8-9880730-4-8

Dedicated to the missing, the silenced,
and the ones we should have seen.

"The missing never really leave us.
They remain, just out of sight."

- Raegan Teller

A Note to Readers

In writing *One for Sorrow*, I sought to portray all characters with care, especially those whose heritage is rooted in the Cherokee people and culture. While this novel is a work of fiction, I approached it with deep respect for the history, traditions, and ongoing presence of the Cherokee Nation.

I am not Cherokee, and I do not claim to speak for the culture. My intention was not to appropriate but to acknowledge, to represent individual characters shaped by their heritage without reducing them to it. I did my best to portray beliefs and experiences authentically.

Any errors are mine alone. I welcome the opportunity to continue learning and listening.

Raegan Teller

One for Sorrow.
Two for fear.
Three black feathers,
And you'll disappear.

CHAPTER ONE

Nothing is more magnificent than the Blue Ridge Mountains in the fall. At least that's what all the travel magazines say. This year, however, the weather had not cooperated. Too much rain had weighed the trees down, and unseasonably warm nights prevented the colors from intensifying. As a result, the fall colors were disappointing—a lackluster display of browns and muted yellows instead of the usual blaze of red and gold.

But Cody Hart didn't care about leaves or what color they were. That's not what had lured him away from Santa Fe, New Mexico and led him to North Carolina. He was on a mission. A personal mission.

Cody followed the directions an old man at the service station had given him and drove until a weathered sign came into view: *Welcome to Raven's Rest.* The man had said it was a small town and that, unlike Asheville, it had come through last year's hurricane with little more than a few downed trees. From the look of it, he'd been right.

His first impression of Raven's Rest was that it was typical of most towns: a small general store, a hardware and fishing equipment store, and dress shop, a barber shop, along with a few vacant storefronts. There was also a small police station, but it appeared to be vacant.

In desperate need for a cup of tea or coffee, Cody decided to try the Raven's Rest General Store. As he entered, it was as though he had stepped through a time warp. A long, well-worn wooden counter held a vintage cash register and a jar of mints with a "20 cents each" handwritten sign taped to it. But a closer look also revealed a small digital register with a touch screen, like the ones popular in all the stores and restaurants now.

"Hi, there. Can I help you?" A woman early to mid-thirties with short, auburn hair was wiping her hands on a dish towel as she stared at Cody.

"I was hoping you might have a cup of coffee or tea, or at least tell me where I can get one," he said.

She smiled as she held out her hand. "My name is Lena, Lena Callahan. I own this place," she said as she waved her arm around the store. "I just made a fresh pot of coffee, or I can make a cup of tea."

"I usually prefer tea, but today I think I need the extra jolt. Coffee's good, black."

"We've got a small eating area in the back." She pointed to a cloth curtain door. "Right through there. Grab yourself a seat, and I'll bring your coffee. How about a bowl of vegetable soup and a couple corn sticks?" When Cody hesitated, she added, "We're the only eating establishment in town. So if you plan to eat anytime soon, we're it."

Cody had hesitated not because he was unsure, but because Lena's smile had captured his attention. It was warm and lit up her face. "Uh, sorry. Yes, soup would be great. I haven't eaten today." Seeing her also reminded him of why he was here, but he tried to push that thought aside, at least for the moment.

Lena threw the dish towel over her shoulder. "Then I'll throw in a piece of apple pie. On the house."

Before Cody could thank her, she had disappeared through the door to the dining area. He followed her, entering a room with wide, worn floorboards, exposed brick walls, and a few tables scattered around the room. A large brick fireplace at the end of the room had several rocking chairs facing it. No fire going yet, as it was too early in the fall.

Cody took a table near the fireplace just as Lena reappeared with a tray. She put a steaming bowl in front of him, a huge mug of coffee, and a big piece of the best-looking pie Cody had ever seen. "I got some vanilla ice cream too if you'd like it."

"No, this is fine. Looks delicious."

Lena hesitated a moment, standing over Cody as if she was waiting for something. "Well, I'll just let you eat in peace. Just call out if you need anything. I'll be in the kitchen checking on some bread in the oven."

The soup was perfectly seasoned with just a slight, spicy kick—but not enough to cause discomfort. As he cleaned the last bite from the bowl with his spoon, Lena came out to check on him. "Can I get you anything else?"

"No, once I finish that pie, I'll be stuffed." As she started to walk away, he called out. "You wouldn't know if there's a place around here I can rent, would you?"

Lena turned and walked back to the table. "You mean like a room, or something more?"

Cody smiled. "Hadn't given it a lot of thought, to be honest. Just someplace I can stay awhile, check out the town, do some hiking"

Lena smiled. "Well, touring the town won't take too long. Guess you can tell we're pretty small. There are several fancy Airbnbs on the outskirts, a little further up the mountain on the river, but they usually stay booked months in advance. Especially this time of year. If you just need a place for a short time and don't need anything elaborate, I've got a cottage out back that I rent occasionally. Nothing fancy, but it's comfortable and clean."

"I'll take it."

"Don't you want to see it or know what it costs?" Lena asked.

Cody laughed. "Why, you going to stiff me, what with me being new in town and all?"

Lena scanned Cody from head to foot, to the point that it made him uncomfortable. "You look pretty strong. You work out?"

"Is that a requirement for renting your place?"

"No, but I was hoping maybe we could work out a deal. I've got some minor handyman work I need done, and I'd be glad to work out an exchange. Would that work?"

Cody grew up on a ranch, so he was no stranger to doing repairs, but he wasn't sure how much free time he'd have. "I'm not really looking for work, but thanks for the offer."

"And I wasn't really trying to hire you, but Buddy, the guy who usually helps me out, tripped over a tree limb and broke his arm trying to catch himself. It's not much work, and it's not a requirement for renting the cabin." She shrugged. "Just thought I'd ask. We can work out a reasonable price, so just let me know when you're ready to check it out."

Cody wiped his mouth with the napkin and swallowed the last bite of pie. "I'll pay my lunch bill now and if you're ready, I'd like to see it."

"I'll just add lunch to your bill if that's okay. You can pay your rent and any food bills at the end of the week. I hate paperwork, so I try to minimize it as much as possible."

Cody stood from the table. "Works for me."

CHAPTER TWO

The cabin was just what Cody had hoped for. One room, with a small bed, a tiny but serviceable kitchen area, a bath, and a decent size closet. Cody pointed to the cooktop. "That's mighty sophisticated for a cabin. Induction burners, right?"

Lena put her hands on her hips. "Well, aren't you the bright one. I mean most men I know wouldn't know an induction cooktop if they fell over it." She waved her hand in the direction of the kitchen. "I installed it because it's safe, you know. Burner won't work unless there's a pot on it. Plus, it heats up lightning fast."

"We, uh, I had one in my kitchen out West."

"I though you looked like you had a little Navajo in you."

"My mom was, but my dad was Irish."

Lena laughed. "That's a helluva combination. As you can tell from Callahan, I'm Irish too. Anyway, there's a few pots under there," she said, pointing to a curtained area under the counter, "and there's a small pantry in case you need to store anything." She pointed to a cracked windowpane over the sink area. "That's one of the chores I need to tend to, but I'll find someone to fix it." She started to leave but turned back. "I'll need to get you a new lock for the door. Someone walked off with it, and since the cabin hasn't been rented lately, I keep forgetting about it. If you need anything, I'm usually in the store, but I also live in the apartment above it." She sighed. "Running that place is 24/7."

Cody took the key, feeling bad about refusing to help her. "That pane won't take long. Just make a list of whatever you need. I'll do what I can, but I'm not sure how long I'll be here. Just want to do some hiking."

"There are some good trails around here, especially by the river. But we've got bears too, so ..."

"I've got a good bit of outdoor experience, but thanks for the warning."

Suddenly, a man burst into the cabin. "Lena, come quick."

"What's wrong? Is someone hurt?" she asked.

"Ayita's gone missing."

Lena's hands flew to her mouth. "Oh, God. Are you sure she's missing?" She looked at Cody. "Sorry, but I need to go. This is Ned, by the way. I'll be back later." She ran out the door and down the path leading back to the store.

"Wait," Lena called out to Ned. "I'm coming with you." But Ned threw up his hand and kept jogging.

Ned headed straight to the town hall, which was just a big conference room at the rear of the bank, where the town's citizens often gathered for meetings. Years ago, Raven's Rest had its own police chief and a deputy, but when the chief died, the office closed for lack of funds. Since the town's crime rate was low, a Wayland County deputy provided their only police presence.

By the time Ned and Lena got to the town hall, a dozen or more people were already gathered. "Are you sure Ayita is missing?" Lena asked.

An older woman called out. "Yes, we can't find her anywhere." She pointed west. "Saw her backpack out there."

"Where's Maker?" Lena asked, referring to Ayita's grandmother. Maker's real name was Cherokee, but since no one could pronounce it, the town began calling her Maker, as she was known for her weaving and sewing skills.

"I'm here." A woman stepped forward from the back of the room.

Lena rushed to her and embraced her. "Maker, I'm so sorry. Has a search party been formed?"

Maker shook her head slowly.

Instead of responding to Maker, Lena looked at an older man in the group and the de facto mayor. "Abe, what are you waiting for? We need to get out there. Now!"

"I'll be glad to help," Cody said. Everyone turned to look at the stranger who had just walked in.

"This is Cody," Lena said as she turned to look at him. "He's staying in my cabin a while to do some hiking."

Most of the townsfolk just nodded or looked at Cody. "I'm pretty good at tracking," Cody said.

"Well, then, let's go!" Lena said and then began giving instructions to those who volunteered to search. "We've got to find her before dark." She turned to Cody. "You come with me. We'll start in the field."

CHAPTER THREE

The field, Cody learned, was an open, flat area, about the size of a football field. Mountains surrounded the area, giving it the feel of an arena. Cody took in the view and pointed to the tree line. "That might be the best place to start."

Lena put her hand on his arm. "I need to fill you in on a few things while we're walking."

Cody nodded and headed toward the trees on the West side of the clearing. "I overheard one of the townsfolk say, 'another one is missing.' Have other children gone missing from here?" Cody felt a familiar and growing tension in his neck, in the same place it always started.

"Mostly from the surrounding areas," Lena said. "Not much to hold young folks here. Sometimes they just want to get away and no one hears from them again. One girl disappeared about a year ago, but she had tried to run away before. But you know, people like their stories, especially in these parts. Supposedly a few kids have gone missing from the surrounding areas a while back. Some say the area is cursed, but it might just be talk. We've got a lot of Native American culture around here, and legends are part of its DNA. And mountain folk also tend to lean into legends and superstitions. Kind of like the Irish, actually."

Cody had heard that explanation too many times when searching for missing kids. *They probably just ran away.*

"What about that guy Abe? He seemed like he was in charge."

Lena made a face. "That's what he wants you to think. He's a bit of a loose screw, if you ask me. His family started this town generations back, after the Revolutionary War. Supposedly, he owns a dwarf donkey ranch further up the mountain. He says those little things sell for about $2000 each." Lena shrugged. "Seems fanciful to me. From what I know about them, they're just pets, too small for anything else. Anyway, people supposedly buy them from all over the country. He claims to make a pretty good living at it."

As they approached the woods, Cody saw something pink on the ground. "What's that?" he asked, pointing.

"Ayita's backpack. They left it here in case she returns. It's supposed to be some kind of bad omen to remove a missing person's things. Keeps them from finding their way back."

As Cody walked toward the backpack, a large black bird spread its wings and perched on it. "Whoa. Now that's a raven."

"They're common around here, and they can get quite large, with wingspans as wide as five feet."

"So that's where Raven's Rest got its name," Cody said. "Ravens are common in New Mexico too. Lots of superstitions around them—good and bad. Some claim they bring good luck. Others say they are signs of something bad about to happen." The bird remained on the backpack, now with its wings spread wide. "Looks like it agrees with you about not messing with the backpack."

Cody and Lena walked around the raven and towards the tree line. Cody kneeled to examine the narrow footpath. "Adult tracks, male. Recent. But no child's. How old is Ayita?"

"Ten. She's fairly small for her age, petite. A beautiful blend of her Cherokee and white heritage."

Cody stood. "Why would she be going through the field? Was she walking to school this way?"

"Ayita is homeschooled, as are many of the kids around here. Nearest school is about twenty miles away, and when the weather is bad during the winter, travel is too dangerous."

"Even without the distance, I can't blame parents these days for avoiding public schools." Cody could sense Lena was studying him.

"Yes, with all the shootings, bullying, and everything else, if I had a kid, I'd homeschool them too. Besides, Maker is a lot smarter than folks give her credit for. I've helped her with a few technology issues, you know, getting Ayita connected online to the school's website, but Maker's sharp when it comes to managing Ayita's schooling."

"I was surprised to get good Wi-Fi reception up here. How's that?"

"We were lucky to be included in the Reconnect Program that was put in place to bring the internet to rural areas. It's not perfect, but it's sure better than satellite—or nothing. More than likely, it was done to boost the tourist trade around here."

Cody pointed west. "They went this way."

Lena looked at where he was pointing. "But that's off the path. Nothing but …" She nodded. "Right, let's go."

Cody stopped a few times to examine the ground and surrounding growth. After walking a short distance, he could hear water. "Is that a river down there?"

Lena nodded. "It's the brink of Whisper Falls, where its descent begins. The crest of the falls is just down that way," she said, pointing. She looked at Cody, tears filling her eyes. "I'm not feeling good about this, you know."

"Let's not jump to conclusions." Cody kept walking toward the sound of the falls. "Did you know Ayita means 'first to dance'?" he called over his shoulder.

"Yes, Maker told me, and it fits her well," Lena said. "That kid is always dancing around, singing. She loves pow-wows and took to learning the native dances quickly." Lena paused. "I pray she's safe. Maybe she just wandered off and got lost."

A short distance later, they were on the banks of the fast-flowing river. Cody looked downstream and could see where the falls began, although the drop-off wasn't deep. A skilled kayaker could easily maneuver over it. He examined the ground. "The tracks end here. And it's just a man's prints, no child's."

"Maybe he was carrying her," Lena said, as her hand flew to her mouth. "Oh, no. I can't believe I said that."

"These tracks may have nothing at all to do with Ayita. Come on, let's look further down."

About fifty yards closer to the crest of the falls, Cody leaned down and picked up a beaded bracelet. "Do you recognize this?" he asked Lena.

Lena sobbed as she whispered, "I helped her make that."

Cody pointed to three feathers arranged neatly on the ground near the bracelet. "Wonder what that's about?"

"One for sorrow, two for fear, three black feathers, and you'll disappear," Lena said so softly Cody could barely hear her.

"Is that some kind of nursery rhyme?"

Lena nodded. "I used to hear Ayita say it. Sometimes she skipped rope saying it over and over." She put her face in her hands and cried.

"Let's not tell the town folks about these feathers for now. Might be important, and we don't want to jeopardize the investigation."

CHAPTER FOUR

Dozens of people searched for Ayita until it got too dark. When all the searchers gathered again at the town hall to compare notes, no one had found a trace of her, except the backpack left in the field and Cody's discovery of the bracelet. Lena showed the other searchers a photo of the bracelet from her phone, withholding information about the three feathers, as Cody had requested.

"Did someone call Deputy Bowen?" Lena asked.

"I did," Maker said, stepping forward. "He came by while you were out and took a report."

"What's he doing? Has he put out an Amber alert?" Cody asked.

One of the townsmen took a small step toward Cody and glared at him, while one of the women gave Cody a slow once-over and smiled. The man beside her said, "We don't get many visitors here, other than those vacation folks who come to the store and do a little shopping. Just kinda funny you show up right when all this is happening." He looked around at the others and added, "Know what I mean?"

"Look," Cody said, "I get that it might seem like a strange coincidence. But that's all it is. I'm from New Mexico. A few friends said the hiking here was worth checking out. I saw the welcome sign, pulled in, and thought I'd explore the town."

The woman who had been staring at Cody, spoke. "And we're mighty glad you did," she said smiling.

"Cody is a skilled tracker, too," Lena said. "That's how he found the bracelet."

The man looked at Cody. "Yeah, that was real handy."

Cody reminded himself they had a right to be suspicious of him. "Look, I know you don't want to move Ayita's things, but they may have DNA evidence that might be destroyed from exposure to the weather." He paused. "What did Bowen say about collecting and preserving them for evidence?"

A few of the townsfolk exchanged glances. One of the other men spoke up. "To be honest, Bowen didn't seem to take this all too serious. He said she'll likely show up when she gets hungry." He looked at Maker and then Lena. "She's wandered off before, you know."

Getting impatient now, Cody turned to Lena. "Where can I find Deputy Tucker Bowen?"

Lena glanced around the room and appeared to be nervous as she took Cody's arm. "Come on, we'll contact him."

When they got back to the general store, Lena confronted Cody. "Alright now, I've defended you, but the truth is I don't know a thing about you either. Who are you, really, and why are you in Raven's Rest?"

Cody smiled. "Well, I guess I've already worn out my welcome."

"Look, I'm a bit testy today. Ayita is, well, special. Not just any little kid. She's had some tough breaks but is smart and talented. And I'm worried." She cocked her head slightly. "Sorry it if seems like we all attacked you. Sit down and I'll make us some coffee, then I'll call Tucker."

"Sure, I could use a dose of caffeine. I usually prefer hot tea, but I drink plenty of both, whatever is available, which is usually coffee." Cody said as he pulled out a chair at one of the tables. "What's this deputy like?"

Lena switched the coffeemaker on. "Tucker's alright. He's good, honest. At least that's my impression." She wiped her hands on a dish towel. "For what it's worth, I agree with you about Ayita's items. They should be protected." She threw the dishtowel on the counter. "I'll give him a call now. My phone's upstairs, so I'll just go up and get it."

While Lena was gone, the coffeemaker signaled the brewing was complete. Cody walked over and pulled two cups from the shelf above and filled his. His hand shook slightly, and an old familiar feeling began to come over him, that feeling that something bad was about to happen. But maybe he was just tired—and a little put off by the resistance he had met at the town hall.

When Lena returned, phone in hand, she had Deputy Bowen on the line. "Hi, Tucker," she said.

Cody noticed the warmth and familiarity in her voice, something he had not noticed in her conversations with him or anyone else.

"Hey, could you come to the store? I'd like to talk to you about Ayita." Then, "Yes, now's a good time. In fact,

I've got someone here who would like to meet you. See you soon."

After her conversation ended, she looked at Cody. "What are you smiling about?"

"Oh nothing. So are you two still a thing?"

"What … no, I mean, none of your business." She slammed the phone on the table. "We're just good friends. But it really is *none* of your business. By the way, he's nearby so he'll be here in a few minutes. Instead of waiting with Cody, Lena went back to the kitchen.

Before Cody had finished his coffee, he heard a voice call out, "Lena, I'm here."

Lena came out of the kitchen. "Wait here, I'll go get him."

Cody could hear her voice, speaking very softly, before the two of them came back to the dining area. Cody stood and held out his hand. "Pleased to meet you, Deputy Bowen."

"No need for formality. Just call me Tucker, like everybody else does."

Cody smiled. "Works for me. I'm Cody Hart."

Tucker was quiet for a moment as he studied Cody. "Say, you look like another fella I met once, he was up here for some kind of police training in Asheville. Can't remember his first name though. Had the same skin coloring, dark hair and eyes."

"You may be referring to Josh Hart. Everyone says we look alike. He and his wife, Enid Blackwell, live in South Carolina. He's the police chief in Madden and she publishes the local newspaper."

"You and Josh related?" Tucker asked.

"He's my cousin. Haven't seen him though since he left New Mexico years ago."

"Well, small world, I guess. Glad to meet you. Lena says you have some questions about the missing girl."

"Ayita, yes," Cody said. "That evidence needs to be preserved."

"Well, folks around here—"

Cody cut him off. "I know the local superstition about not moving a lost person's items, but as an officer of the law, you've got an obligation to preserve the evidence."

Tucker put up his hands as if surrendering. "Whoa there, Hart. Are you suggesting I'm not doing my job?"

Lena stepped between them. "Look, guys, let's not make this a pissing contest, okay? We're all after the same thing—to get Ayita back safe."

"Fine with me," Tucker said, looking at Cody. "May I ask who you are and why you're interested in this case?"

"I didn't know Ayita, and I've no connection to anyone here. I came here to hike in this area and rented Lena's cabin for a short time. But I've worked more than a few missing persons cases, mostly hikers, and there's no time to waste. And that evidence could be critical if she was kidnapped."

"Kidnapped? That's a giant leap forward. You a cop?" Tucker asked Cody.

"I'm on leave from my job as a special agent for the US Forestry Service in New Mexico."

Lena looked at Cody. "It would have been nice if you had mentioned that earlier."

Cody shrugged. "Didn't think it was relevant. I'm not here officially, just another tourist."

"Must be nice to take an extended vacation to hike," Lena said.

Cody turned to Tucker. "Shall we go get those things?"

"As you said, Hart, you're out of your jurisdiction, and I don't particularly want you meddling in this case. I'll talk to the townsfolk and then go out in the morning to get the backpack."

"There was a bracelet by the river also." Lena pulled up the photo on her phone and showed it to Tucker. "That's the one I helped her make."

Tucker put his hand on Lena's arm. "I know you two were close, but don't worry. We'll find her."

"An Amber alert would be nice too," Cody said.

"Of course. Anything our *unofficial* friend wants, I'm happy to oblige." He and Lena exchanged looks. "I'll head over to the town hall now," he said to Lena.

CHAPTER FIVE

After Deputy Tucker Bowen left the general store, Lena poured another cup of coffee for herself. "Want another?" she asked Cody.

"No, I'm good."

"Oh? I've got some hot tea, or maybe even a beer or two in the fridge."

"Thanks, but I'm good." He took a deep breath and then added, "Look, I'm sorry if I caught you off guard about my job. I honestly just didn't think it was a big deal."

"You're right. It's not a big deal. Folks around here are just spooked, that's all." She took a sip of coffee. "I wish I could say it's because these kinds of things don't ever happen here."

"Oh? Is there more to that comment?" When Lena didn't answer, Cody continued. "You mentioned some local legends earlier. You know, most of the time, legends have some basis of truth, even if they become embellished over time." He smiled. "Tell me about the legend of Raven's Rest."

"As I said, I wasn't living here then, but years ago a girl disappeared from a nearby town. So keep in mind that I'm just sharing stories I've heard."

Cody nodded. "Got it."

"Like Ayita, the girl was part Cherokee. At that time, there was a school bus that picked up the Raven's Rest kids and took them about twenty miles down the road to the nearest school. The funding for that bus got cut years back, as I understand it, which is one reason why most of the kids are homeschooled now. That plus all the bullying, especially for Native Americans. At that time, the easiest way to get to the main road was to cut through the field."

"Do you remember her name, the missing girl's?"

Lena shook her head. "No, but someone in town can probably tell you. I'm sure Abe would know."

Cody smiled. "As suspicious as they are of me, I'm sure they'll be annoyed if I ask too many questions."

"Anyway, she didn't come back on the school bus that day, and the driver said she never got on that morning. The town traced her steps and found her jacket along with one of her schoolbooks in the field."

"Sounds eerily similar. I'm starting to get a bad vibe about this field," Cody said. "Did they ever find her?"

Lena shook her head. "As far as I know, she was never found."

"Any suspects, maybe locals with an interest in young girls?"

"Not that I'm aware of." Lena leaned back in her chair and sighed. "You know, it's a funny thing about small towns, especially mountain towns like these that are somewhat isolated from the rest of the world. I can tell you absolutely that if I needed anything or was sick and couldn't take care of myself, these folks wouldn't hesitate to help me."

"But?" Cody asked

"But I'll always be an outsider."

"So why do you stay here?" Cody asked.

Lena stood and gathered her coffee cup and napkin. "That's a long story. Maybe later."

Cody reached out and put his hand on her arm. When she stepped back slightly, he quickly withdrew his hand. "Sorry, I didn't mean to … my apologies. And I'm not trying to pry into your personal life. Just trying to get a handle on this town." He paused. "How did Raven's Rest get its name?"

Lena eased back into her chair. "Well, as far as I know it's been called that since it was founded around 1800. It was established by Revolutionary War veterans seeking land grants as a reward for their service."

"If I remember my history lessons, North Carolina became a state about the same time," Cody said.

"That's right, you must have been a good student," Lena said smiling. "The state's constitution was ratified in 1789, at least that's what the plaque at town hall says. Abe claims his family started the town, and no one has ever challenged that," Lena said. "Abe says they took the name Raven's Rest because so many of them were seen around here."

"So, the child you mentioned that disappeared before Ayita, was that the only one?"

Lena stood again. "You need to talk to someone who grew up here. That's all I know." She hesitated briefly. "I've heard a few rumors about girls from further up the mountain going missing, but it might just be talk. I think some of them just leave. Not much to hold them here."

As she got up abruptly to walk to the kitchen, Cody called out, "Did I upset you again?"

"No, I'm just worried about Ayita, and rehashing old

legends won't help. I got enough of that from my Irish family growing up."

Cody sat at the table a few moments thinking about Lena's comments and wondering if Raven's Rest held secrets that might help them find Ayita.

CHAPTER SIX

The next morning, Cody went to the kitchen where Lena was stirring a pot at the stove. "Good morning," she said. "Just putting on a stew for lunch." She wiped her hands on a dish towel and turned to Cody. "Look, I know I was a bit bitchy last night, and I'm sorry. It's just that—"

"No need to apologize. Here I am a stranger in town, taking advantage of your hospitality and being too nosy for my own good. I'm the one who should apologize."

Lena smiled slightly. "Let's call it a draw then." She motioned toward the coffee pot. "Just brewed." She turned to Cody. "Oh, but you said you prefer tea. Sorry."

"No problem," he said, as he reached into one of the pockets of his hiking vest and pulled out a tea bag. "Got any hot water?"

"There's an electric kettle over there," she said pointing. "That's an odd-looking tea bag you have."

Cody held up the small bag made from cheesecloth and string. "It's a blend I order from a friend. Want to try one?"

Lena shook her head. "Not now, maybe later."

When the kettle beeped, Cody poured the water over the bag in his mug. "If I get in trouble today, will you bail me out?"

"From that mischievous grin on your face, I assume you're going to be asking a lot of questions." Lena put her hands on her hips. "Are you married?"

Cody almost dropped his mug. "Where did that come from?"

Lena looked at Cody, as if sizing him up. "There's something about you that makes me think you are. Or at least you were."

"I'll make a deal with you. When we're both ready, we can share our stories. Until then, you can rest assured no angry wife is going to come storming in here to accuse you of anything. Deal?" Cody hated being secretive, but he barely knew Lena, and he had to be cautious of who he trusted here.

Lena shrugged. "I guess so." She wiped her hands again. "I'd start with Maker. She'll be more cooperative. But she's going to grill you, much worse than I have." She paused. "And Abe will be upset you didn't ask him, if he finds out.

"That's okay. I think I can take it." He finished his tea and took the mug to the sink and began washing it out."

Lena took the mug from his hands. "I'll get this. You're still a guest, albeit an annoying one at times. And I take care of my guests. Now get out of here."

Smiling, Cody turned to leave, calling out over his shoulder, "Yes, ma'am."

By 8 am, there was already a handful of people at the town hall, including Abe. When Cody entered the small building, all eyes turned to him. "Morning, folks," Cody said. "Mind if I join you?"

No one welcomed him, so he just walked over and sat in one of the empty chairs. The woman who had eyed him top to bottom yesterday smiled. "Any news on Ayita?" Cody asked.

"Nah," Abe said.

Before Cody could respond further, Deputy Tucker Bowen walked in. "Morning," he said. His eyes settled on Cody. "I see you're back to help us out."

"May I say something?" Cody asked.

"By all means," Abe said, "share your wisdom with us."

Cody stopped himself from saying something he might regret later or responding to Abe's sarcasm. "I realize you all think me being here is a bit strange, given the timing. But I assure you, my only interest in Ayita's disappearance comes from my background as an investigator in similar cases. That is, lost people in rugged surroundings. And I know you all care about her." He glanced around the room but didn't see Maker, her grandmother. "I'm offering to help, but if you don't want it, then I'll just do some hiking and get out of your hair."

The woman who was obviously his fan addressed the group. "For Pete's sake, y'all. Why in the hell are you giving this man such a bad impression of this town? He's got the experience to help us and we should accept it." She turned to Tucker. "No offense, Tucker, but we all know you're not a tracker or an investigator. Can we please put this pettiness aside and get on with finding Ayita?" She sat down and crossed her arms across her chest.

Maker walked in, poured herself a cup of coffee, and sat near the back of the room. Silent nods were offered in her direction as she passed.

Cody resisted the urge to thank his admirer. She might be a hopeless flirt, but she was an ally.

Abe grunted and pointed at Cody. "We're taking you at your word because we're good people. But …"

Cody didn't need for Abe to finish the sentence. He got the message: screw up, mister, and we'll throw you out of town. If Cody didn't have a bigger reason than hiking for being in Raven's Rest, he would have left. Instead, he walked over to where Tucker was standing and put out his hand. "Let's work together. How can I help you?"

Tucker paused momentarily before shaking Cody's hand, offering no comment. Instead, he turned to the group. "We've put out an Amber alert, and Mr. Experienced Investigator here wants me to secure the backpack and bracelet for evidence." And then he muttered, "Even though we don't know if this is a crime." Tucker glanced at Cody to emphasize the jab.

Before anyone else could respond, Maker stood up to speak. "I'd like to say something. I know we have all honored the tradition of not moving anyone's things when they're gone. But that tradition was meant for when people had just left, like going off to war or going missing from a hunting trip." Her voice choked. "Ayita is a child, and if this man," she said, pointing to Cody, "has experience finding people in the woods, then we need to listen to him and let him help. If he thinks they can find anything on the backpack and bracelet to help find my baby girl, then I'll go get it myself." She then turned to Tucker. "Put your ego aside, Tucker, and work with him. He seems to be a good man, and he has some sorrows too. I can see it in his eyes.

If he's willing to put that aside and help us, then I thank him for overlooking our rudeness." She sat down again.

For what seemed like a long time, but only a few seconds, the room was silent. Tucker then turned to Cody. "Alright then. Let's get going. I brought evidence bags."

CHAPTER SEVEN

Cody and Tucker walked together in silence toward the field. After a few minutes, Tucker said, "Look, man, I'm sorry if I—"

"You're doing what I would have done," Cody said. "I'm a stranger in town, showing up just when a child disappears and offering to help. As we both know, perps often insert themselves into an investigation to get involved. We're good, okay? Let's just agree to put our rocky introduction aside."

Tucker smiled slightly. "Truth is, I'm glad to have your help. I'm not a mountain man, as Maker said." Tucker waved his arm around the area. "Mountains feel claustrophobic to me, make me feel boxed in."

"I read an article once that some people feel exactly like you do about the mountains," Cody said. "I, on the other hand, feel vulnerable and exposed when I'm on a beach. I miss the protectiveness of the mountains. But other folks feel free and liberated staring out at the ocean. Guess it takes all of us to make the world interesting."

Tucker snickered again. "Yeah, I grew up in Charlotte and then transferred here to Wayland County because I wanted something different. But then I realized I don't like bugs, bears, or snakes. I can mostly avoid them though. Usually don't have much reason to go in the woods."

Cody laughed. "I get that. After a day of tromping

around the forests of New Mexico, all I wanted was a cold beer and a long, hot shower—in that order." Cody stopped walking and put his hand on Tucker's arm. "Look, I'm not here to make you look bad or to steal your thunder. I have no reason to impress anyone here. And I'll be gone in a couple weeks at most."

"I appreciate you saying that. But I think Lena's already impressed with you."

"I'm just a new person in town, and she's curious. That's all."

Tucker snickered like a teenager. "Okay, man, if you say so."

"Speaking of Lena, she was telling me a little about the legends around here—and about a child who went missing over a decade ago. You know anything about that case?"

"Nah. I heard about it, but I'm not sure about the details."

"But they never found the girl?" Cody asked.

Tucker shrugged. "Not as far I know. But I've only been working this area a little over a year. And, if I'm honest, I hope it won't be another year."

Cody patted Tucker on the back. "So if we can solve this case, maybe you'll get promoted and can move back closer to the big city. That way you can work on car thieves, drug dealers, bank robbers, pimps—the usual good stuff."

Tucker chuckled. "Now we're talking."

Suddenly, Cody put his hand on Tucker's arm. "Shh."

"What—"

Cody put his finger to his lips. "Shh." He pointed

ahead and began slowly walking toward a large tree, motioning for Tucker to follow behind him.

Tucker put his hand over his holstered gun, whispering. "What? What do you see?"

Silently, Cody looked around and then walked over to the large tree, its trunk hollowed out over the years. He pulled a small flashlight from his pocket and examined the void inside the tree. "Someone was recently in here. Perhaps sleeping," Cody said softly.

"Do you think it was Ayita?" Tucker asked. "Maybe she hid here."

Cody examined the area again. "No, this was an adult, large. Probably male." He studied the leaves and twigs around the area and then motioned for Tucker to follow him.

They walked in silence for several minutes. "This way," Cody said, pointing.

"That will take us to the river."

"I know," Cody said. "And that's the way he went." Leading the way, Cody picked up his pace and walked until the sound of the river became louder. "The tracks end here."

"You think he jumped in the river?"

Cody couldn't stifle his smile. "No, I think he pulled a kayak into the river." He pointed to the damp ground.

Suddenly, Tucker pointed to an area in the smooth dirt near the drag marks. "Is that what I think it is?"

Cody kneeled to the ground. "A child's footprint."

Before Tucker could respond, a noise behind them made him whirl around. "What was that?" he asked.

Instead of responding to Tucker, Cody pulled a can of

bear spray from his backpack and starting yelling.

"Was that a bear?" Tucker asked. And then added, "I hate bears."

"I saw some tracks back there," Cody said. "And black bears are common in this area." He looked at Tucker. "You know anything about them?"

Tucker shook his head. "Not really. That's one of the reasons I don't go into the wooded areas often." He patted his gun. "Not without this."

"Well, as a lawman, you likely know that shooting a bear is a serious offense. Besides, there's no need to. They're more afraid of you than you are of them."

Tucker snickered. "I doubt that."

"Seriously. They're looking for food, water, and space. If they try to attack, it's because they feel threatened."

"Someone told me to lay down and play dead."

"Must have been someone who knows nothing about black bears. They aren't like grizzlies. Playing dead won't save you from a black bear. First rule: don't run because it triggers their chase instinct. And trust me, you won't outrun a bear. Stand your ground, make yourself look bigger—arms up, jacket open. Talk to it, firm and steady, so it knows you're human, not prey."

"And if it keeps coming?" Tucker asked.

"Back away real slow, no sudden moves. If it charges, bear spray's your best bet—aim for the face."

"And if it actually attacks?" Tucker kept staring at the woods.

"Then you fight back. Hard. Go for the face, the snout, whatever you can reach. Make it regret coming after you." Cody looked around the area. "Come on. I think it's gone back the other way now. Let's walk the riverbank and see if we can tell where that kayak came back to shore. And then we need to collect that backpack and bracelet to get it analyzed for DNA or other evidence. By the way, where are the search parties?"

"There are two search parties out. They went in the other direction since we were coming here. One party is some of the younger folks in town, and the other group is from Weaverville. They came over to help once the word got out."

"Maker didn't seem too emotional about all this. Do you find that odd?" Cody asked.

"Yeah, I know, but she's not an emotional woman. I don't think I've ever seen her really upset. And these people around here seem to take things in stride. I had to get used to it myself when I first started working with them. But I guess it wouldn't help anything for her to get hysterical." Tucker met Cody's gaze. "You think Ayita was kidnapped, don't you?"

"I don't know, but in my experience, you assume the worst and work from there." Cody slapped at an insect on his neck. "One thing for sure, Ayita didn't take that kayak in the river by herself. She's with someone, voluntarily or otherwise."

CHAPTER EIGHT

After walking thirty minutes along the river's edge, Cody said, "There's no way to continue along here. Too much growth close to the water. And the water's too deep for wading." He pointed downstream. "What's down there? Any houses near the river?"

"There are several cabins nearby, mostly Airbnb rentals," Tucker said. "Some folks stay for a night or two, others longer."

"You probably should go talk to them. See if they look or act suspicious, or if they noticed any suspicious activity lately," Cody said.

"I was planning on that. I'm not totally clueless, you know. In fact, I'm a good deputy, just not an outdoorsy type."

"Sorry, no offense meant. You ready to head back and pick up that evidence?"

Tucker nodded.

"Can I ask you a question?" Cody asked, pulling a piece of paper from his backpack. "You recognize any of these people?"

Tucker took the paper and studied it. "Might be easier to tell if you had an original photo. This copy isn't too clear."

"The originals are back in New Mexico." Cody pointed to a cabin in the background of the photo. "Do you recognize this place?"

Tucker held the paper closer to examine it. "Looks like a cabin that was burned out. Don't know when though. It was like that when I saw it."

"Where is it? Can you tell me how to get there?"

Tucker just looked at Cody, studying him. "You're not really here to hike, are you?"

"Sure I am. Just found this photo in an album back home and got curious. Figured it was in this area."

Tucker took a long look at Cody again. "I might not be a fancy tracker and investigator like you, but I'm not stupid." He kept staring at Cody. "How do I know you're not some crazed killer out here stalking more victims?"

Cody smiled. "I'd say you've been watching too many movies." He crossed his arms across his chest. "Look, I'm not here to cause problems, for you or anyone else. Just trying to find a family member, okay? One day we'll come out here to the river with a six pack and I'll tell you all about it." Cody held out his hand. "Deal?"

"Sure, whatever," Tucker said, ignoring Cody's hand. "You know there are a couple of open cases around here. Missing people that were never found. You looking for one of them?"

"No, the person I'm looking for disappeared from New Mexico. And I'm probably grasping at straws to be looking for … to be looking here." Cody stretched his arms in the air to release the sudden tightness he was feeling in his neck and shoulders.

"Well, I hope you find whoever you're looking for. When we get back to my car, I'll show you on the map where that cabin is, or where it was. Might be leveled and cleared away by now."

"Come on, I'll show you where the bracelet is," Cody said.

"I feel sorry for Maker," Tucker said as they were walking. "That girl is her whole world."

Cody put his hand on Tucker's shoulder. "If she's alive, we'll find her."

"Lots of places out here to get rid of a body," Tucker said. "I don't have a good feeling about this. And all these creepy stories about Raven's Rest gives me the willies."

"What kind of stories?" Cody asked.

Glancing around nervously, Tucker said, "Probably just talk, that's all."

"I'd like to hear the stories, even if they are just legends."

"You'd probably need to talk to Maker. I've just heard a few, but she knows 'em all. Come on, let's get out of here before more bears show up."

It's not the bears we have to worry about, Cody thought.

CHAPTER NINE

It was getting late in the day by the time Cody and Tucker got back to Raven's Rest. Tucker had collected the backpack, bracelet, and feathers and said he would turn them over to the sheriff. "They'll likely send them to Asheville or Davidson for processing, you know, better equipped labs. Won't be quick, though."

"Have you called in a canine unit?" Cody asked.

"They were supposed to be here today but a couple of hikers went missing and the nearest unit was deployed. They'll bring the dogs tomorrow."

Cody nodded, although he was concerned about the seeming lack of urgency. "Can you tell me about that cabin now, the one in the photo I showed you?"

Tucker motioned for Cody to follow him to the black SUV that had a Wayland County Sheriff's Department emblem on the door.

"Nice ride," Cody said.

"Yeah, it's alright. Weather can get nasty up here during the winter, so we have to be prepared." Tucker pulled a paper map from the inside pocket of the door.

"Haven't seen a paper map in a while," Cody said. "Old school, I like it."

Tucker laughed. "Sometimes GPS doesn't work up here, and it doesn't show all those dirt side roads I sometimes have to take. You can tell this map is pretty old. Got it from the guy who covered this area before me."

Cody examined the map, which had pencil notations all over it.

"There," Tucker said pointing to a road on the map. "That's where I think that cabin might be, or was. But I can't be sure. You might want to show that photo to Maker or Abe. They can probably be more helpful."

Cody took a photo of the area on the map with his phone. "Thanks."

"Don't forget, you owe me that beer." And then Tucker added, "And some answers."

Cody watched as Tucker drove away from town and then walked up the path to the cabin to take a shower. But before he could get inside, Lena stopped him.

"I'll bet you're hungry," she said.

"You know, I forgot I haven't had lunch. A bowl of that stew and a beer would be great."

"You look like you need a shower first. Come on to the store when you're ready."

Cody sensed immediately something was different about the cabin when he walked in. But what? He glanced around and then noticed that the papers he had left on the small table had been rearranged. Or had they? Maybe he was just getting paranoid.

Cody brushed his concerns aside and after showering, put on fresh jeans and a sweater. The late-fall weather was turning cool, especially after dark.

He walked the short path to the general store and

could already smell Lena's stew. "Man, that smells good," he said as he walked into the dining area. "Didn't realize how hungry I was until just now."

Lena smiled as she placed a large, steaming bowl at the place she had set for Cody. "We've got a pretty good selection of local craft beers. Thought you might like this one." She put a bottle on the table, its label showing the name: The Dweller.

"That's an interesting name for a beer."

"It's made by the Green Man Brewery. Has hints of chocolate and coffee in it."

"I love it already," Cody said as he took a sip. "Don't think it would take many of these to put me under, though."

"Stout beers always seem heavier. I guess it's my Irish upbringing and love of Guinness that makes me partial to them."

Cody held up his bottle in a toast. "Here's to the good ol' Emerald Isle and the lovely lasses it produces."

Lena leaned in slightly. "Flattery won't get you out of paying the rent, mister."

"Oh shucks, it usually works," Cody said. "And this stew is outstanding." He took another bite and then asked Lena, "Mind if I ask you something?"

She sat down in the chair opposite him at the table. "Sure. Go ahead."

He pulled the paper copy of the photo from his jeans pocket. "Tucker pointed me to where he thinks this might be." He pulled out his phone and showed her the map. "Have you seen this place?"

Lena leaned back in her chair. "You know, I was just

beginning to believe your story about coming here to hike. But now …" She ran her hand through her short hair. "I remember seeing it somewhere. Maybe it was in a newspaper article. But I can't remember much else about it."

"According to Tucker, it burned, and he wasn't sure what, if anything, would be left of it." He paused. "And for the record, I'm not trying to be mysterious. I found it in some family photos, and I thought if I was coming here anyway, I might check it out." Cody watched Lena's face, hoping he had sounded convincing. "I can ask Abe or Maker."

"I'd ask Maker, if I were you. Her memory is better than Abe's."

"Thanks." Cody folded the paper and stuck it back in his jeans. "I wanted to talk to Maker anyway."

"About?" Lena asked, and then before Cody could answer, she added. "Sorry. It's none of my business who you talk to or about what or why. You know, when you live in a small town, it does something to you. Strangers come in, and instead of being glad for a new face, we all start wondering what they're up to. You must think we're terrible. But like I said before, basically these are all good people."

Cody took the last sip of beer from the bottle. "Small towns, or even communities within a large city, are all the same in that way. You have every right to question why strangers show up, but I promise you I'm not here to harm anyone." He glanced at the old schoolhouse style clock on the wall. "I've got a few things to do before I go to bed, and I'm a bit tired. Out of practice from the days when I walked trails all day." He laid the crumpled paper napkin in his empty bowl. "I'll be glad to help you clean up the dishes. I'm pretty good at it."

Lena stood and snatched up his plate. "I told you, you're a guest. If you need more blankets, there's some in the cabin on the top of the closet. One of Maker's quilts is up there, and it's really warm." She gathered up the rest of the dishes and left Cody sitting there alone.

CHAPTER TEN

Cody was typically an early riser, but he had slept longer than usual. He loved the mountains and would have liked nothing more than to live in a cabin by a river, fly fish and grow a little garden. But only if Nora was by his side. As he lay in bed, he heard bloodhounds baying in the distance. He had always admired their ability to follow a scent and find people, but if Ayita's trail ended at the river, the scent would end there too.

He stuffed a couple of Ezra's tea bags in his vest pocket. Ezra was an elderly man who lived in the mountains of New Mexico. He came from a long line of medicine men, although Ezra himself didn't practice. Or so he said.

Cody and Ezra had fished together many times while sipping some of Ezra's homemade wine that was strong enough to curl your toes. Even though Ezra didn't identify himself as a medicine man, he was known around the area for his healing teas. Some tasted like grass, some were bitter, and some, like the tea Ezra gave Cody, tasted amazing—more like a commercial herbal tea. Ezra insisted that Cody drink it, because he claimed it would make him wiser than his enemies and therefore keep him safe.

Cody was only partially Native American, on his mother's side. His father disappeared not long after Cody was born and was supposedly white. Since Cody had never met his father, he never missed him. Nor had he ever seen a photo of him. Thankfully, he had uncles and male cousins who helped raise him and taught him to fish and hunt, along with other survival skills.

But being raised by a single mom had given Cody a different view of the world. She was kind, patient, and wise beyond her years. All she wanted was for Cody to marry a good woman who would love him—nothing else mattered. A good woman, his mother said, was an angel sent by God to keep men from messing everything up. He smiled as he recalled their conversations.

Cody had married a good woman. But now she was gone.

He pulled on his jeans and grabbed a fresh sweater from the closet. As he walked down the path to the store, he hoped Lena had gotten over being upset with him. He didn't like being secretive, and he'd likely tell her more later.

When he walked into the store, he saw a cup, a carafe of hot water, and a plate, napkin and silverware at the table, which he assumed was for him. Lena did a good lunch business, and from what he could tell, had a decent breakfast crowd also. But this morning, the diner was empty. Perhaps they had gotten up earlier to join the search.

"Good morning," Lena said, walking toward Cody. "I made pancakes. They're in the oven. Been there a little while, so I hope they haven't dried out."

Cody glanced at his watch. "It's only seven thirty. How early do you folks get up?"

Lena shrugged. "Search parties went out just after sunrise. Since they left, I've been making cakes for the church bazaar coming up Sunday. They auction them off to help pay for repairs to the building."

"You still upset with me?" Cody asked.

Without answering, Lena went to one of the cabinets and pulled out a handful of papers. She walked back to the table and threw them in front of Cody. "Like to tell me about this?" Cody didn't have to pick up the copies of newspaper articles to see what they were. His wife's photo was under the headline: "New Mexico Woman Disappears."

For what seemed like an eternity to Cody, neither he nor Lena spoke. He wasn't sure what to say, but eventually replied, "I see you've been doing some research." It sounded colder than he intended.

"Hiking, my ass. I knew you were up to something else."

"I just wasn't ready—"

Before he could finish, Lena cut him off. "I trusted you. I gave you a place to stay." She took a deep breath. "You were suspected of killing her. Do I have a murderer staying in my cabin?"

This was not the way Cody had hoped this conversation would go. Given the easy access to information on the internet, he was foolish to think a smart woman like Lena wouldn't run a background check on him. And now she felt betrayed.

"I'm sorry for withholding information, but I didn't lie to you. And I certainly had nothing to do with Nora's disappearance." For a few seconds, he studied the room, randomly taking in every detail of the dining area while gathering his thoughts. "She is the love of my life. A good woman, and I miss her." He quickly brushed his eyes with the back of his hand. "More than I can bear at times."

Lena sat down in the chair beside him. "Look, I'm sorry I came on so strong. But I knew something was up with you showing up like this in our little town." She paused. "I didn't expect this," she said, pointing to the articles. "If you want to talk about it, I'm a good listener."

Cody nodded and looked away for a moment. "About a year ago, I was out on the trail looking for two missing hikers. Nora did volunteer work for the Aurora Path Foundation that helped runaways get back home or, if needed, she'd arrange counseling since some of the kids came from abusive homes and didn't want to go back."

Lena listened intently, while nervously fingering a dish towel. "So how did she go missing?"

"She had said she wasn't feeling well that morning when I left and that she might call in sick. So I called her about nine o'clock to check on her, but she didn't answer. I just figured she had taken something and was sleeping off whatever bug she'd caught. I called again about an hour later and still no answer, so I called our neighbor and asked her to check on Nora."

"I'm sure you were worried."

Cody nodded. "It was almost noon when we found the lost hikers, and they were in an area with no cell reception. So I didn't know what was going on with Nora. As soon as I got into an area with cell service, I called again." Cody's mouth had suddenly gone dry and his temples were pounding, as he recalled the panic of those moments. "When I called our neighbor again, she said Nora was nowhere to be found. Nothing was missing that she could tell, and Nora had not taken her purse or phone. She'd simply vanished."

"And that was about a year ago?" Lena asked.

"Yes."

"And no word from her since then? Do you think she just left on her own?"

"No. I mean anything is possible, but why leave without any money, credit cards, or phone?"

"Was there any sign of a fight, anything knocked over?" Lena asked.

"No. I left everything as it was for the deputies to see. They ran fingerprints on everything, but the only prints they found were hers, mine, and a few neighbors who regularly came over."

"But why would they suspect you? Had you been fighting?"

Cody smiled slightly. "If you watch any detective shows, you know the spouse is the first suspect. I took a polygraph and passed it, but after a few months with no clues as to what happened, I guess they wanted to close the case. So they came after me with a vengeance. Since I was alone in an area with no cell reception at the time of her disappearance, I couldn't prove where I had been that morning. After a month of questioning by my superiors, digging through our financial records and anything else they could, they finally admitted I was not a suspect. But by then the papers had gotten wind of it and wouldn't let it go. Some local podcaster started a series on Nora's disappearance and during one episode brought up the fact that I had come from a broken home, so therefore I couldn't possibly have had the perfect marriage I claimed I had, because obviously I wouldn't know what that was like." Cody ran his hand through his hair. "It was maddening."

"So you think she came here? I mean that photo of a cabin you showed me last night, what was that about?"

"I have no idea how, or if, the cabin is significant. At this point, I'm grabbing at straws. But I do know she had some relatives in North Carolina, supposedly not far from here." He paused briefly. "She mentioned several times that she'd like to visit them because she had little family left."

Lena put her hands on her hips. "And that's it? She's been gone a year, and you came across the country from New Mexico to North Carolina because of a photograph and a few casual comments?"

Cody sighed loudly and stared at the ceiling. "After a year, the case went cold, and then I found out Nora had been helping a runaway teenage girl. She had been held captive in the North Carolina mountains and managed to escape."

"What? Held here, in Raven's Rest?"

"I don't know exactly where, but it was near here, according to the woman who told me. Supposedly, the girl told Nora she was terrified of ravens because of her experience here."

CHAPTER ELEVEN

After hiking around the area most of yesterday and wandering about the nearby areas, Cody had a good night's sleep, the first in many nights. He had avoided the search area by walking back toward the highway, away from Raven's Rest. The fresh air and time alone, as well as getting away from the town briefly, were just what he had needed to clear his head.

Cody texted Tucker that he would join the search party later, as he had something to do first. Despite their earlier friction, Cody could tell Tucker wasn't happy about going back into the woods alone.

According to Lena's directions, Maker lived not far from the town limits, down a dirt road. And while Maker made the walk into town nearly every day, Cody decided to drive to save time.

When he got to her cabin, Cody was amazed at the style of her place. It was not a mountain-style cabin as he envisioned, but a one-story cottage with curtains at the window and a garden in front, looking more like Maine than western North Carolina. Before he got to the front door, Maker opened it and motioned for him to come inside.

"Saw you coming up the road," she said.

"I would have called you, but Lena said you don't have a phone."

Maker laughed and pulled a cell phone from her pocket. "I do, but I don't tell most folks, and Lena is sworn to keep my secret." She put her fingers to her lips. "Now you have to swear too." She directed Cody to have a seat in a large, upholstered chair, and she sat in a wooden chair across from him.

"Nice place," Cody said.

"I grew up in various cabins, so I was determined to have a real house, a flatlands house." She motioned toward the kitchen. "Got some herbal tea brewing in the kitchen. Would you like a cup?"

"Sure." Cody took in the details of the living area while Maker was getting the tea. There was only one photograph with a young girl, who he assumed was Ayita.

Maker set a large steaming mug on the table in front of Cody. "Here you go. I drink it neat, but I've got some honey if you'd like it."

"No, neat is fine. I'll just let it cool a bit."

Maker sat back in her chair and eyed Cody. "Been expecting you to drop by."

"Why's that?"

"You got troubles that brought you here, I can see it. So why don't we just cut to the chase, and you tell me why you're here and what you need from me."

Cody sipped the tea to buy a few seconds of time. Her directness had caught him off guard, and he wasn't sure how to respond. "That's really good. Honestly, I was expecting it to be bitter. You make the blend yourself?"

"Nah, it's store bought. Republic of Tea," she said laughing. "I gave up making my own years ago. This is much better."

Cody laughed. "So much for stereotypes."

"You Navajo?"

"Partly, on my mother's side," Cody said. "You're Cherokee, right?"

Maker nodded. "Mostly. Lots of marrying across lines these days, so many of us are like this tea. You know, a bit of this and a bit of that." She stared at Cody again. "So, you going to answer my questions?"

Cody pulled out the copy of the cabin photo he had shown to Tucker and Lena. "Do you know where this is? And who owns it?"

Maker pulled a pair of large pink reading glasses from her pocket. "Can't see much without these. Ayita picked them out. Said they were 'cool.'" She smiled slightly. "I sure miss her." She held up her hand. "But let's not talk about her until I figure you out." She studied the cabin photo. Yeah, I know it. About ten miles up the mountain. Far as I know, Abe's family owns it, bought it from the previous owners. But they own a lot of property around here." She handed the paper back to Cody. "What's that got to do with you?"

"Did you know the previous owners of the cabin?" Cody asked.

Maker shook her head. "Nah. It was before my time here." She squinted slightly. "I'm waiting for some answers from you."

Cody gave her the same information he had given Lena. As he talked, he studied Maker's face for any clues about what she might be thinking. But she was expressionless, her eyes deep, dark pools, not giving anything away.

"So you think your missing wife is here, or hereabouts? Is that your story?" Without waiting for answers, she continued. "And this is because you found a photo of this cabin, your wife had relatives hereabouts, and she was helping someone who's afraid of ravens? That's it?"

Cody was not surprised Maker had the same reaction Lena had. "Yeah, that's about it."

"I'll give you directions to get to that old place, but it burned years ago. After the fire, word is that Abe bought the cabin for nearly nothing. I always wondered about that, you know, have convenient it was for him to get a good price. But I doubt there's anything there to help you find your wife." She stopped again to stare at Cody. "What about that girl, the one who was kidnapped?"

"That's all I know." Cody saw a reaction on Maker's face for the first time. "Do you know anything about that, a kidnapped girl from around here?"

Maker shrugged. "Heard some stories. That's about it." She fingered the edge of her apron, as her eyes filled with tears. "You know, there are a lot of stories about missing kids. Some may be just myths and legends. The mountains seem to encourage folks to make up tales." She wiped her eyes with the back of her hand. "As you can tell, there isn't much to Wayland County. Never was. Folks say it's the land the world forgot, but I say it's the land that never asked to be remembered. This here was Cherokee ground long before you or me, back when the mountains still spoke a language we forgot how to hear." Maker stared off into space for a moment before continuing. "You know the legend of Raven's Rest?"

Cody shook his head.

"So the story goes, Ravens gather just before someone disappears."

"But there's a lot of ravens around here," Cody said." How could you tell if they are gathering or just, well, just a bunch of ravens?"

"According to the legend, they leave three feathers as their calling card, a kind of warning."

"One for sorrow, two for fear, three black feathers, and you'll disappear," Cody said.

Maker sat up in her chair. "Where'd you hear that?"

"Lena told me."

Maker leaned over and put her hand on Cody's arm. "Tell me the truth. Did you find three feathers out there looking for my Ayita?"

Cody saw fear on Maker's face for the first time. "Yes, by the river, where we found her bracelet."

Maker shook her head and buried her face in her hands. "Another one."

CHAPTER TWELVE

After leaving Maker's house, Cody decided to visit the cabin in the photo. She said it was about ten miles away. That wouldn't be far in the city, but Cody knew driving ten miles in the mountains could take much longer than usual. He texted Tucker to see if they had found anything or if there was any news about Ayita. Nothing. "Has the sheriff considered calling in the state police?" Cody asked.

"He said he might. The sheriff doesn't much like to call in the North Carolina State Bureau of Investigation. He says they try to take over."

Cody was familiar with the territorial possessiveness of local law enforcement and their jurisdictions. "You've been looking for several days. It might be time to put that aside and call in the SBI."

"Not my call. You coming on the search today? The signal's pretty iffy up here. Gotta go."

Cody started down the road, following the directions Maker had given him. It was a straight shot, but the road was narrow and full of deep potholes from Helene, the hurricane that flooded the rivers in the western mountains of the state. It was going to be a long, difficult ten miles.

By the time Cody reached the cabin, which he easily recognized as the one in the photo, he was tired and aching from the rough ride. He parked his pickup in front of the cabin.

The front wall and two sides were still standing but heavily charred. The right side had collapsed, either from the fire or from neglect.

Carefully, he stepped over the threshold into the shell of the cabin. After studying the layout of the small structure, he decided the right side must have been a bedroom area and appeared to be the epicenter of the worst damage. There was enough left of the kitchen and living areas to identify their purpose. A stone fireplace in the living area looked like it had been used recently, probably a hunter or some kids had decided to build a fire. A wooden walking stick, crudely carved at the top with some kind of animal, leaned against the side of the stone fireplace. Cody took the stick to steady his walk through the debris laden floor and to poke around for any critters that might be hiding.

Most of the roof was intact in the living and kitchen areas, but as Cody carefully made his way into the right side, the roof had collapsed and littered the floor, making walking in the bedroom area difficult. He poked at the piles of charred wood on the floor with the stick, hoping to find something, but all he found was more burned wood.

Cody was preparing to leave and declare this search a waste of time, but something caught his eye in the debris. He poked at the pile with the stick until the object was visible. It appeared to be a cloth tote of some kind. Using the end of the stick, he pulled at the object until it was free.

The tote looked like the kind used for groceries or gym clothes, nothing fancy. Yet, something about it seemed familiar. Where had he seen a tote like this, or at least a similar one? Then he remembered. When he was cleaning out the garage one day, he'd found a box of green cloth totes and asked Nora what they were for. She said they were given to the runaways to keep their meager belongings in. Green, she said, was the color of personal growth and of healing. She had put them in the garage after an event and had forgotten about them, saying she would take them back to the Aurora Path Foundation.

Cody tried to remember if the totes were the same shade of green as this one. *Don't jump to any conclusions.* Ever since Nora had gone missing, he saw connections everywhere. But he was desperate for something, anything that would give him answers.

Once Cody had steadied his nerves, he studied the tote more closely. It was not burned or even smoked, so it had been put there sometime after the fire. He looked inside and found a receipt for a meal, breakfast most likely from the food items listed, and a Busbud brochure. A number was scribbled on top, and Cody was relieved that he didn't recognize it as Nora's handwriting. Or at least he didn't think it was. Had he ever paid attention to how she wrote numbers?

The wind was stirring outside, and Cody decided it was time to get out of this nearly destroyed cabin and go back to town. He put the items back in the tote bag and folded it in half, sticking it under one arm. After returning the walking stick to its place beside the stone fireplace, Cody walked back outside. The sky was getting dark, hinting at a thunderstorm on the way.

When he stepped into the open area in front of the cabin, he heard a rifle shot nearby. Probably just someone hunting or target practicing in the area.

The drive back to Raven's Rest was downhill all the way, but it wasn't any easier. It was hard to see anything in the rearview mirror with the dust cloud behind him, but at one point, he saw a Jeep Wrangler not far back. It kept its distance, so he couldn't say for sure it was following him, but he had an uneasy feeling. By the time he got to Raven's Rest, the Jeep had disappeared into the dust.

CHAPTER THIRTEEN

Since there was a little more daylight left, Cody decided to track down Tucker and see how the search was going. He texted but after five minutes there was still no reply. He walked down the path to his cabin and put the tote under his mattress.

Lena had warned him about Abe, which didn't surprise Cody. He knew that small towns usually had strong hierarchies, a definite pecking order that wasn't to be violated. He wanted to talk to Abe and would try to be sensitive about Abe's de facto leader status.

Cody figured Abe was either at the town hall or in Lena's store, so he changed into fresh clothes. Lena was wearing an apron with red apples embroidered on it, which made him smile for some reason. Probably because it seemed out of character for her, or at least his impression of her.

"I like the apron," Cody said.

Lena turned around from the stove with a big wooden spoon in her hand. "Thanks. Ayita and I worked on it together. Took us for-ev-er," she said, drawing it out. "Neither of us are very good at embroidery."

"Well, I could tell it right away they were apples, so there's that." He sat down at one of the tables. No one else was in the dining area, but it was still early. The supper group usually arrived around six or seven in the evening.

"You ready to eat? This stew needs at least another twenty or thirty minutes."

"Actually, I came in hoping to find Abe, but I didn't look at the time," Cody said.

Lena sat down at the table beside him. "About that. I wouldn't tell him you've already talked to Maker."

Cody couldn't stop himself from grinning. "Am I in big trouble? Is the town going to tar and feather me? I read somewhere that's how North Carolina became the Tar Heel State."

"You can laugh if you want to, but this town is already on edge with Ayita's disappearance, and they don't need a stranger coming in here messing with their ways."

Cody tilted his head to one side. "You keep saying 'they' instead of 'we.' Why's that?"

Lena pointed a finger at him. "You think you can just change the subject on me instead of answering. Well, it won't work."

"Look, I'm sorry. I just felt like talking to Maker. And it was productive. I found the cabin in the photo."

"And?" Lena asked.

For a moment, Cody wanted to tell her about the green tote bag but decided to keep that to himself for now. Besides, it would sound ridiculous for him to draw a connection between Nora and a discarded tote in a burned cabin nearly across the country from where she was last seen. "The cabin was easy enough to find."

Looking frustrated with Cody's lack of meaningful information, Lena stood and walked back to the stove. "Abe's probably down at the town hall. He thinks he's running the search teams.

Just as Lena suggested, Abe was sitting at one of the meeting tables in the town hall looking at a map of the area. He glanced up when Cody walked in but then turned back to his map.

"Hey, Abe," Cody said. "Mind if I sit a minute?"

Abe looked up slowly. "I'm busy. What do you want?"

"I won't keep you long. Just wanted to ask how the search is going and see if you need for me to do anything."

"Seems like you been busy today. Enjoy your ride up the mountain?"

Cody wasn't sure how to respond. Had Maker told him about the photo of the cabin? But then, it was pretty hard to sneak around in this town. "Rough roads, but it wasn't too bad. I guess your family owns a lot of land around here?"

"My family founded this town."

"So I've been told. You must be proud. That your cabin up there, the one that burned?"

Abe made a noise like a horse exhaling air. "That what you came here to ask me?"

"Well, no, I wanted to see if you knew anything about a missing girl, a teenager, that disappeared from this area little over a year ago. I don't know if she lived in Raven's Rest or just in this general area."

Abe leaned back in the wooden chair, which made a squeaking noise under the shift of his weight. He was a big man and had likely been formidable in his prime. Now what was left of his hair was silver, and he was carrying at least thirty pounds more than he should. "I'm still wondering if it's a coincidence, you showing up here right about the time Ayita went missing." Abe leaned forward, scowling. "You get why I'm curious?"

"Well, I had hoped we were past that, but, yes, you're a prominent citizen in town, and I've raised your suspicions. All I can do is assure you I'm here to hike." And then added, "And to help if I can."

"You hadn't done much of that, now have you, Mr. Hart. Hiking, I mean. Seems you've spent your time sightseeing."

"I've been trying to make myself useful with the search. But if you'd rather I not help, just say so."

"Why you asking about that other missing girl?" Abe might not have meant to, but he just confirmed the incident.

"My wife works with missing kids. I was just curious, that's all." Cody didn't mention that a girl from this area had shown up in New Mexico.

"She wasn't missing. She ran away. That girl was trouble, liked to make up lies." Abe drummed his fingers on the table. "If you know where she is now, I'd like to let her family know."

"I don't know. As I said, my wife is the one who worked with her."

Abe shifted his weight, causing another groan from the chair. "Where's your wife, the one you keep mentioning?"

"She couldn't make the trip but she wanted to, especially since she has some distant relatives around here."

"You don't say?" The crease between Abe's eyes deepened. 'You're just full of coincidences, now aren't you?" Abe turned back to his map, making it clear the conversation was over.

"I'll help Tucker again in the morning, unless you object."

Abe made another grunting sound. "That boy. He's as out of place as a …" Abe stopped short of finishing.

"Tucker's alright." Cody said. "But I'll try to teach him a few survival skills."

Abe scowled again. "Yeah, you do that, Mr. Investigator."

Cody left the town hall and made his way back to the store, then followed the path to his cabin. When he got there, the door was slightly ajar. He hadn't locked it because Lena hadn't replaced the missing lock yet. Besides, she said they had never needed locks in Raven's Rest, which is why Cody carried his phone, wallet, and copies of Nora's photos with him in a backpack, no matter where he went.

Deciding he probably hadn't closed the door completely, Cody stepped inside without hesitation. But then he saw the lights were on, and he was positive he had turned them off before leaving earlier.

Looking around, he realized his mattress had been moved, as if someone had hastily put it back in place. Also, the drawers to the small chest were partially pulled out, and the freezer door was open. Police often checked the freezer for hidden drugs or other illegal items, and if Cody had been searching this cabin, he would have looked there too. But why would someone else do so?

Cody's puzzlement then gave way to anger. He was with Abe, so that eliminated him. Cody walked over to the bed and lifted the mattress. The green tote was gone. Why had he left it here? But who would want it and why? For someone to take the tote meant his instincts were right about its significance. Someone didn't want Cody to have it.

Cody stomped down the path to the store. Lena was serving in the dining area, so he waited until she returned to the kitchen. "We need to talk as soon as you're off work."

She studied Cody's face. "What's going on?"

"Let's talk later." Cody stormed out of the store, causing several people to stare at him.

When he got back to the cabin, he texted Tucker to call him. Cody then laid across the bed, closing his eyes and trying to connect the dots. Undoubtedly, the break-in, if you could call walking into an unlocked cabin breaking in, was a result of his poking around at the burned cabin earlier in the day. When Lena came to talk, he'd ask her about the gray Wrangler that followed him. Perhaps it was a coincidence. Cody smiled when he recalled his conversation with Abe. Maybe Abe was partially right. Maybe Cody was so desperate to find Nora that he was imagining these coincidences.

He closed his eyes and tried to ease the tension in his neck and shoulders. Nora wouldn't have left him without saying something. Surely she knew he would be sick with worry. More than ever, Cody was convinced she was in trouble. And it had something to do with Raven's Rest.

CHAPTER FOURTEEN

By the time Lena came to the cabin, Cody had dozed off to sleep. The weight of Nora's memory was wearing him down.

"Cody?" Lena said softly. "Cody?"

Cody woke to her gentle prodding. "Are you alright?" she asked.

"Sorry, I was a bit tired and fell asleep."

"I had one piece of chocolate meringue pie left, so I tucked it away for you." She put the small plate wrapped in tinfoil on the table. "And I brought you come hot tea to go with it."

Cody sat up and tried to regain his alertness. "That was nice of you, thanks." He paused. "Look, I'm sorry for my outburst earlier."

"What was that all about anyway?" Lena asked.

"Come sit with me while I dig into that pie." He pulled a chair out for her at the table that was only large enough for two.

Lena sat, looking at Cody as though studying his face would provide her with answers.

Cody took a big bite of pie. "This is really good." He wiped his mouth with the napkin Lena had supplied. "Someone broke into the cabin while I was at the town hall. Well, actually, they just walked in. But the place was tossed."

"So that's why you were upset with me." She lowered her head a bit. "Because I didn't put a lock on the door. I'm sorry, and I'll take care of it in the morning." She glanced around. "Did they take anything of value?"

"No." He debated whether to tell her about the tote.

"Well, that's good. Could have been kids. With all the Airbnbs popping up around here, we get a lot of teenagers visiting the area. I don't worry about the locals."

Cody was certain vacationing kids didn't want a weathered green tote bag, but he kept that thought to himself. "Perhaps." He took the last bite of pie, scraping the plate with the fork. "Do you know anyone around here who drives a dark gray Jeep Wrangler?"

"I don't think so. But we have a good many vacationers coming to the store this time of year, and I don't pay much attention to what they drive. Why do you ask?"

"Just wondering."

Lena stood up. "Now look here. These questions you're asking and then someone coming into the cabin, I want to know what's up. You're not being honest with me."

Cody reached out and gently tugged at her arm. "Sit down. Please."

Lena returned to her chair.

"I can see your Irish roots coming out," Cody said. "Remind me not to get you really mad. But you're right. I'm not telling you everything."

"Because you don't trust me?" Lena asked.

"To be honest, my thoughts are all over the place. But you, yes, I trust you. I just don't want to put you in a position of withholding information, should anyone ask. If I tell you, though, that's exactly what you'll have to do—keep it to yourself."

Lena's face reflected her confusion. "You're making me a bit nervous. Now I'm not sure I really want to know what's going on with you."

Cody remained silent to let her words sink in. If he told her what he knew, would he place her in danger? But was it fair to stay here, renting her cabin under false pretenses?

"Go on," Lena said. "Tell me."

"Are you familiar with the name Baxter Greene?"

Lena's eyes widened. "Yes, I've heard that name. She lived not far from here. I heard she ran away several times after she got caught stealing. But what's she got to do with you being here?"

"Well, it seems she turned up in New Mexico at the Aurora Path Foundation. My wife Nora was working with her."

Lena put her hand to her mouth. "How on earth did Baxter get to New Mexico?"

"According to one of Nora's friends who works at the center, Baxter caught several rides with long haulers, in exchange for a few favors along the way."

Lena shook her head. "Poor girl."

"According to Nora's friend, Baxter claimed she left home because she was being abused by a family member."

"So I guess she didn't want to go back," Lena said.

"Exactly. Nora was helping her find a place to stay and arranged for her to get counseling."

"Nora sounds like she was, sorry, I mean *is*, a kindhearted soul," Lena said patting Cody's hand. "I'm sure you're worried sick about her. But I don't understand how helping this girl Baxter in New Mexico put your wife in danger. That's nearly across the country. And how does that explain why you're here?"

"According to the folks at Aurora, Baxter was planning to go on to California, 'where dreams come true,' she said. Apparently, she was about to leave New Mexico and continue west when she was picked up for stealing a sandwich from a convenience store. The police released her in the care of Aurora if Baxter promised to stay there and get counseling. The woman who told me all this said Baxter became very upset about something while she was there, but she wasn't sure what. And it was just before Nora disappeared. The woman thinks it's because one of the truckers Baxter had ridden with, and had confided in, was from around here and knew the Greene family. And as luck would have it, the trucker told the family where she was headed after he found out who Baxter was."

"Damn. Poor kid couldn't catch a break," Lena said softly. "So you think all this is tied to Nora's disappearance?"

Cody ran his hand through his hair. "Honestly, I'm not sure of anything any longer. But it can't all be coincidence." Cody looked away briefly, gathering his thoughts. "I guess no spouse can ever be a hundred percent sure about their marriage, but I had no reason to think Nora was unhappy."

"It's so sad to think of kids having such a bad home life that they would rather live on the streets."

"And obviously, there are always opportunists ready to take advantage of these boys and girls," Cody said.

Lena blinked away tears, cleared her throat, and changed the subject. "You mentioned you had a conversation with Abe. How'd that go?"

"Not great. I think he knows there's more to my story than I've told him, and he has a right to be suspicious. If I were in his shoes, I'd be suspicious of me too. And I think he had me followed today."

"Where did you go? To that old cabin in the photo you asked about?" Lena asked.

Cody nodded. "I poked around in the part of the cabin that was still standing and found a green cloth tote bag."

Lena looked confused. "And?"

"And I was followed by a gray Wrangler coming back down the mountain. When I got back here, I put the tote under my mattress. As far as I can tell, it was the only thing taken by whoever came."

"Wait, I'm totally confused. You found a green tote bag, and then someone followed you to get it back? That sounds beyond crazy, you know."

"Not when you consider that Aurora Path Foundation gave green totes, just like it, to the kids they worked with." Cody clenched his fists involuntarily. "And Nora used them a lot too. She said one can never have too many totes."

Lena's hand flew to her mouth. "Oh my." She put her hand on Cody's and then withdrew it. "But why do you think Abe had you followed?"

"Because he knew I was at the cabin today, and unless Maker told him, that's the only way he could know about my interest in the cabin—from whoever followed me."

"Was there anything in the tote?" Lena asked.

"Just a receipt from a restaurant and a Busbud brochure."

"Isn't Busbud that company that makes bus reservations?"

Cody nodded. "Maybe Baxter had planned to catch a bus at some point to continue her trip to California. There was a phone number written at the top of the brochure, which I was going to check out. But I don't remember the number at all."

"I told you Abe's a bit of an oddball. He thinks he owns this town, and his family does own a lot of property around here. But this is … Well, I'm having a hard time believing he's behind any of this." Her voice lowered. "I can see where he might have you followed, but …" Lena chewed on her lower lip. "You think Ayita has been taken, don't you?"

Before Cody could answer her, his phone rang and he glanced at the screen. "I left a message for Tucker earlier. Do you mind if I take this?"

Lena stood. "I need to get back anyway. We can talk more later."

Cody waved to Lena as she left and then took the call. "Hey, Tucker. Thanks for getting back to me. Any update on the search today?"

"Well, I did find out something interesting, and I'd like your thoughts on it." Tucker paused. "But I'd rather tell you in person. You coming to the search tomorrow?"

"Planning on it. Where can we meet up?" Cody asked.

"I'll text you in the morning, around 6:30 am. I want to get an early start. That work?"

"Sure," Cody said. After the call ended, Cody wondered what Tucker meant by 'interesting.'

CHAPTER FIFTEEN

Lena had begun serving breakfast at 6 am, an hour earlier than usual, for the search parties who needed to get an early start. Cody had a couple of scrambled eggs and an order of Lena's homemade sourdough bread, toasted and slathered with butter. Funny how things he probably wouldn't have eaten in New Mexico tasted much better here. Maybe it was because of the fresh air. And if he had to be honest, getting away was what he needed, at least temporarily. Too many memories of his and Nora's life there. Every time he thought of her, his chest tightened. Was she alive? Dead? In pain? Being held captive? The questions had taken on a life of their own, constantly gnawing at him, day and night. Never giving him any peace.

"Need a refill on that tea?" Lena asked. "Got some hot water and a fresh tea bag right here." She opened her hand to show an herbal tea bag, just like the one Maker had given him.

"I see you've been talking to Maker. Or did you just coincidentally have the same kind of tea she served?"

Lena smiled. "She might have mentioned I should stock them. Got one of my Asheville friends to drop some off when she visited yesterday."

"That was thoughtful. Thanks."

"Maker really likes you. And she's pretty good at sizing people up."

"I like her too. But there's something going on with her. Can't put my finger on it."

Lena laid the tea bag on the table. "That's what happens when you're a cop. Everyone looks suspicious."

"You're probably right."

Lena returned to the kitchen and Cody checked his phone for messages and the local weather forecast. It was 6:35 am. Why hadn't Tucker texted? Assuming he had likely just forgotten, Cody messaged him and then put the fresh tea bag in his cup.

At 7:00, Cody has still not heard from Tucker and was getting a little irritated, so he decided to go find him. Outside the store, Cody recognized one of the men who was part of the search team. "Hey, you seen Deputy Bowen this morning?"

The man shook his head. "We were supposed to go out together again today, but I haven't heard from him, so I'm going with another group."

"You were with him yesterday?" Cody asked.

The man nodded. "Pretty much all day. Why?"

"Which area were you searching?"

"We rode out to an area several miles from here. I don't think a ten-year-old would walk that far, but Tucker said he had something he wanted to check out."

"What was around that area?" Cody asked.

"It used to be a campground. You know, the kind church groups book for outings, Scout trips, and things like that. Far as I know, no one has used it for years. Heard the state seized it because of the back taxes owed. But who knows if that's true."

"Who owns it now, do you know?" Cody asked.

The man shrugged. "No idea."

Cody mentally registered that bit of info in his memory to check out later. Might be useful, might not. "Can you tell me how to get there?"

"We didn't find anything, but I'll show you where it is. Tucker dropped me off and said he was going back there again. Something about a white truck we saw. Just came in, turned around in the field, and left. I just figured he was lost. Easy to lose your way on these roads if you don't know them." The man took Cody's map and pointed to the area, showing him which roads to take."

"Thanks," Cody said. "By the way, do you know anyone around here that drives a gray Jeep Wrangler?"

The man shrugged. "Wranglers are popular around here, you know, four-wheel drive and all that. And gray's a common color." The man rubbed his stubbled chin with his hand. "Mind if I ask why you're interested?"

"Just curious about someone I saw. That's all. Thanks for the directions. And if you hear from Tucker, tell him to call me."

CHAPTER SIXTEEN

The old campground area was about five miles from town, and the unused roads had developed deep potholes that made for slow going. By the time Cody got to the area the searcher had pointed out, Tucker had still not contacted him. He searched for the number of the county sheriff's office and called the number. After a few rings, a young woman answered.

"I'm trying to locate Deputy Tucker Bowen. Is he in, or do you know what section he's working today? I was supposed to join him to search for the missing girl from Raven's Rest, but I seem to have missed him."

The woman expressed sympathy for the lost girl but said Deputy Bowen may have been pulled off the search and assigned elsewhere. She wasn't sure though.

"If that's the case," Cody said, "he would have notified me. I need to talk to him."

The woman asked Cody if she could put him on hold while she checked with someone else. When she returned, she said no one had heard from Bowen and they assumed he was in Raven's Rest. She said they would try to locate him and would relay Cody's message.

Cody ended the call, but it didn't end his questions. He didn't know Tucker well, but the young man seemed sincere enough and not the kind of person who would pull this kind of stunt intentionally. That now familiar feeling of tenseness and dread washed over Cody.

Standing beside his pickup, he looked across the area that had supposedly been a campground. The open area looked a lot like the one where they had found Ayita's backpack, except bigger.

Nature and the passage of time had reclaimed much of the area, which was now covered with small pines and other growth. Hearing a familiar sound overhead, Cody looked up and saw a group of ravens circling the area, behaving more like vultures. From a conversation with one of the elderly men in town, Cody had learned that a group of ravens is called an "unkindness" or a "conspiracy" of ravens, which he thought was interesting.

He looked up at the ravens and called out, "What unkindness did you see? And what secrets are you conspiring to hide?" He was beginning to understand why these mysterious birds often appeared in folklore.

The ravens' calls intensified as they swooped lower, their harsh, guttural kraaawk kraaawk echoing across the clearing like an ominous chant. A medley of throaty rak rak calls and sharp clack clack noises layered over one another, creating a chaotic, almost sinister symphony.

"Tucker," Cody called out as loud as he could. Overhead, the ravens continued to circle. Cody began walking to an area about twenty yards away, where the ravens seemed to be gathering overhead.

Suddenly one raven left the others, gliding through the sky like a shadow and landing on a pile of limbs and debris a few feet ahead. Ravens were also common in New Mexico, and Cody knew they often have a body length of more than twenty inches and a wingspan of close to five feet.

"What is it?" he asked the raven, feeling a bit foolish. "What are you trying to tell me?" The raven began making a clack clack sound and flapping its wide wings. Suddenly, the raven flew away to join the others overhead.

Cody walked over to where the raven had perched. He grabbed a stick lying nearby and used it to poke at the pile of debris. The dead limbs on the pile appeared to have been deliberately placed there—not randomly scattered by wind or weather.

The early signs of insect colonization were unmistakable. Even in the cool Appalachian autumn, the sweet, acrid scent of death had summoned its first responders with uncanny speed. Metallic green blow flies, common to these mountains, clustered and buzzed around the edges of the leaf pile, drawn in by the odor of decay. These Lucilia flies—and their blue and black iridescent cousins—are often the first to arrive, sometimes within minutes, laying eggs in less than an hour on bodies in the open air.

Cody crouched beside the pile, the scent catching in his throat. He'd found bodies before, usually strangers. But Tucker, though ... this was different. Cody knew from his experience looking for lost hikers, fugitives, poachers, and others who sought to hide out in the rugged Santa Fe National Forest, that nature usually wins.

But this was not an act of nature.

CHAPTER SEVENTEEN

As Cody watched the black coroner's van leave the old campground, he thought of the life Tucker would never have, the kids he would never raise. The woman he would never love.

From the condition of the body, Tucker had likely been dead since sometime yesterday. But why had he come back here?

A deputy walked over to where Cody was standing. "Mind if I ask you a few questions?"

"Sure." Cody grimaced involuntarily as he remembered those words. *Mind if I ask you a few questions about your wife?*

"I'm Deputy Freeman. You're the one who found the body, right?"

Cody nodded.

"Mind if I ask why you decided to search this area? It's a little out of the way, don't 'ya think?"

Cody knew that question was coming. "We had been searching together, and we were supposed to meet up this morning. After I didn't hear from him, I asked another searcher in town where he and Tucker had been looking yesterday." Cody patted his vest. "Got a map in the pocket, here. Mind if I pull it out to show you?"

Deputy Freeman nodded, and Cody produced the map. "Here's where the guy told me they had been searching. And he said Tucker said he wanted to go back and check something out, perhaps about a white truck they saw."

"Who was this man you talked to, the one who told you about this place?"

Cody rubbed his neck with his hand. "Sorry, I'm not from this area, just here to do some hiking. I'm staying in Lena Callahan's cabin. Don't know the guy, but he's in one of the search parties. I can probably find out."

Freeman smiled. "That Lena is one fine gal, she is. And does some of the best cooking around." His smile then faded. "But what made you go to that particular pile of rubbish? There are several scattered around here." He made a sweeping gesture with his arm.

The ravens showed me. "Just saw a bunch of birds around it and got curious, started poking around."

"You seem to know your way around the woods, eh? Most folks wouldn't come up here alone."

"I'm a forestry service special agent, on leave. I spent most days tromping around in areas other people wouldn't, or shouldn't, go."

"Hmm. Mind giving me your ID?"

Cody reached into his backpack and pulled out his New Mexico driver's license and credentials, which he handed to Freeman. "Here you go."

Freeman looked at the license, took a photo with his phone and handed it back to Cody. "You vacationing here?"

"Just took some time off to hike the area." Cody knew if Freeman did any checking on him at all, he would discover Cody's wife was missing—and that Cody had been a suspect, at least for a short time. "My wife, she went missing about a year ago. She may have had some family here, and I'm just trying to find out what happened." Cody paused. "You can verify all this with the forestry service in New Mexico." Cody put his identification back in his wallet and pulled out a business card. "Here's the man to call."

Freeman studied Cody again and took a photo of the card. "You gonna be in Raven's Rest a while longer?"

"Not sure, but I won't leave without checking in with you first, if that's your concern." Cody glanced back up to the area where he had found the body. A forensics team was doing a thorough search and taking photos. "Mind if ask about Tucker's family. Do they know?"

Freeman kicked at a small rock with his shoe. "Probably shouldn't say this, but you being a lawman and all, I guess it's okay. Tucker's parents have been notified. His mom's got cancer, took it real hard." Freeman cleared his throat. "How about we go back to town and find that guy that worked in this area with Deputy Bowen yesterday."

CHAPTER EIGHTEEN

By the time Deputy Freeman and Cody got back to Raven's Rest, people had gathered at town hall to talk about Tucker. While the official cause of death had not yet been announced, everyone knew Tucker's death was no accident.

Cody pointed out to Deputy Freeman a man sitting with several others. "That's him. That's the man that worked with Tucker yesterday."

"Come on with me," Freeman said to Cody.

Freeman walked up to the man and introduced himself. "Need to ask you a few questions, if that's alright."

The man looked at Cody then back at Freeman. "Sure."

"I understand that yesterday you and Deputy Bowen worked in the area where we found him, that right?"

The man nodded. "Most of the day, yeah."

"Mr. Hart here," he said motioning to Cody, "he says you told him Deputy Bowen wanted to go back to check out something in that area. That right?"

Again, the man nodded. "He said something about new information, but I didn't pay a lot of attention. I didn't think a kid would wander up that far. That's rough country—bears and … well, just not a good place for anyone, much less a child."

"But you went up there with Deputy Bowen anyway,

right?" Freeman asked.

The man nodded.

"Do you remember anything at all about what he may have discovered that caused him to go back there?"

The man shook his head. "Just that he seemed interested in a white truck we saw. I figured they just took a wrong turn off the county road and got lost."

"Did he get a plate number?"

"I don't think so, but I can't be sure. I hate what happened. He went back up there after he dropped me back off in town yesterday afternoon. Maybe I should have gone with him, but …"

"You don't need to feel bad about any of this," Freeman said. "We're just trying to get a timeline and find out what made him go back there."

When Freeman asked the man for his ID in case he needed to contact him again later, Cody excused himself. Lena was sitting with Maker and was visibly upset, so Cody walked over to them. "Lena, I'm sorry. I know you and Tucker were friends."

Lena sobbed. "What's going on around here? Why is all this happening?"

Maker took her hand and held it.

Cody often asked "why?" But there were usually no answers. Looking at Maker, Cody asked, "Someone told me the area where Tucker was found belonged to Sonny, Ayita's father, at least at some point. You know anything about that?"

Before she could answer, Abe walked up. "I see you got yourself another coincidence, Mr. Hart. Guess it was just luck, you being the one to find the body and all."

Maker looked up at Abe. "That's enough."

Abe shrugged and walked away.

"I'm sorry for his rudeness," Maker said. "Abe is a bit off sometimes, says things that don't make sense."

"It's fine. Besides, he's got a point." He looked at Lena and wanted to comfort her in some way but couldn't think of what to say or do. "I seem to be in the middle of everything since coming here. As I was asking when Abe walked up, does Ayita's father own that land?"

Maker made a face and grunted. "That man laid Ayita's seed, that's all. He's no father and he wasn't a husband."

Cody waited for her to continue.

"Lot of folks around here are land rich and cash poor. Back in the day, land could be bought for nearly nothing, and some people grabbed it up. But time and taxes caught up with 'em and they've either sold to developers or anyone else willing to take it off their hands."

"What about the field where Ayita's backpack was found? Who owns that land?"

Before answering, Maker stared at Cody an uncomfortably long time. "That's sacred land, not that anyone around here remembers what that means. It's owned by no one … and by everyone."

CHAPTER NINETEEN

Cody hadn't slept much last night. Thoughts of Nora, Ayita, and the fresh image of Tucker's body drifted through his mind like smoke that wouldn't clear. At dawn, he gave up on sleep and brewed himself a cup of tea.

Nora had once said to him that he was a "solver." But this puzzle and how all the pieces fit together was too elusive. All the hints and incomplete information were driving him crazy. And Lena was too upset over Tucker's murder for him to discuss it with her. If he couldn't find answers in Raven's Rest, he'd have to look elsewhere.

He hadn't decided whether to trust Maker. Until last night, he felt comfortable. But her demeanor had changed drastically when he began quizzing her about the old campground where Tucker was found.

Deputy Freeman had given Cody his card that included his cell number, so Cody texted him to let him know he'd be in Asheville for the day. No point in throwing more suspicion on himself by disappearing.

Freeman texted a reply telling Cody to be sure to return to Raven's Rest. Cody sighed. *Would I have told you I was leaving if I wasn't planning on returning?* Cody reminded himself that Freeman was doing exactly what he would have done. It was just damned uncomfortable being on the other side of the law for a change.

The drive to Asheville took about an hour. It was

pouring rain and traffic was slow. The largest library in Buncombe County was the Pack Memorial Library in downtown Asheville. He had reserved computer time and made it just in time to claim his spot. He signed in and began searching property records. He didn't have an address for "the field," which made it difficult to find.

He did find the history of Raven's Rest, which listed Abe's family as the founders, but after an hour of frustrating searches, his computer time was up. While much of law enforcement, including the forestry service, used technology extensively, Cody rarely relied on such tools. He left that part to others who were available if he needed anything researched. Whereas in the field, Cody was the expert. The vast wilderness of the forest was his domain. Realizing he needed help, he went to the service desk and asked for assistance.

The woman at the desk was attractive and petite, with dark hair and an olive complexion. "May I help you?" she asked, carefully pronouncing each word with a slight accent.

"Ma'am, I need to find out some information about a piece of land in Raven's Rest. Unfortunately, I don't have an exact address. Is there any way you can help me?"

She smiled and pointed to the name tag on her sweater. "I'm Mira. Let me see what we can find out." She left and came back with a large book open to a map of the area. "Is it here?" she asked, pointing to Raven's Rest.

"Yes, exactly." Cody put his finger on the map. The field I'm looking for is about here, outside the town limits."

Mira slid on thick rimmed, oversized turquoise glasses

and leaned over the map. "This is strange," she said, glancing up. "You are not the first person to ask me about this field."

"You mean someone else asked about this specific location?" Cody asked.

"Yes, I think so. I remember it only because he first asked one of our student volunteers, and she was unable to help him, so the girl came to me for help."

"Do you remember who it was, I mean was he a local? A developer? Real estate agent?"

"You know, I am remembering our conversation a bit more now. Like you, he wanted to know more about the land and its history."

"Did you get the impression he was a local?"

"I don't remember. Wait just a minute." She left the service desk and returned shortly, holding a Portage reporter's notebook in her hand. "I keep notes for all the requests, just to help me remember while I'm doing research. It wasn't that long ago, so it should be in this notebook."

"Were you a reporter?" Cody asked.

Her face beamed suddenly with a large smile. "Now, I remember. He asked me about this notebook too, and whether I was a reporter. He was a crime podcaster, from Raleigh, I think. But I cannot be sure because I did not write that down."

Cody had wondered how long it would take the press to get wind of Ayita's disappearance, but he should have realized that these days, amateur podcasters were the new press, often showing up at crime scenes and attempting to insert themselves into investigations. But many of them lacked the formal training of trained journalists, as well as the ethical standards and duty of care needed on sensitive cases. He'd had to deal with his fair share of these pseudo reporters during investigations in New Mexico, as well as the podcaster who had irresponsibly reported on Nora's disappearance. Journalists he knew and respected complained that overzealous podcasters sometimes blur the lines between advocacy, entertainment, and journalism—and lack editorial oversight. But in all fairness, as Nora had often reminded him, true-crime podcasts have, at times, influenced real cases, sometimes reopening cold investigations or swaying public opinion.

"Well, I guess we'll hear his episode soon enough," Cody said, pointing to the notebook. "So, you never said. Were you a reporter?"

Mira shook her head. "No, I was not. I studied English, then got a masters in Native American folklore. That is how I ended up in Asheville after I graduated. But sadly, I couldn't find a way to make a decent living with my degree." She shrugged. "So I am here now, helping good people like you."

She flipped back a dozen or so pages in her notebook. "Here. This is it." She pointed to a specific note. "And I remember now. He said he was doing a podcast about a child that disappeared from that very place, the property you are searching for."

"Did you make a note of what you found?" Cody asked.

Mira nodded. "Yes, I did, in case he came back later." She pointed to the note again. "The property is owned by a trust managed by an attorney in Columbia, South Carolina.

That is all I have written here." She pulled off her glasses. "I know this area you are looking at a little from my school research. It is full of stories, legends, and folklore."

"Do you know anything about that particular piece of land?" Cody asked.

"As I recall, that parcel of land, known locally as 'the field,' as you mentioned earlier, was a sacred place where Native Americans gathered each year to celebrate various spiritual events. Kind of like Stonehenge."

Cody remembered Maker had also said the land was sacred. "But if so, why is it just an overgrown field now?"

Mira smiled. "Folklore tends to fade away as the people who held those stories die. Younger people do not value the same things as those before them. It is sad in a way." She shrugged and held out her hands, palms up. "So that is why we study these stories and try to preserve them."

"That's interesting, thanks. By the way, any chance I can get a little extra computer time?"

Mira pointed down the hallway. "Go down to the reading room. I will give them a call to give you thirty minutes more. Will that work?"

Cody thanked her and walked down the hall. The woman at the desk pointed out the computer, and with a stern look, reminded Cody there would be no more extensions to his computer time. If he needed more, he'd have to come back later.

After thirty fruitless minutes, he sat back, staring at the blinking cursor. An empty, overgrown field in the middle of nowhere, once sacred ground. Now hidden behind a trust.

CHAPTER TWENTY

After another night of tossing and turning, Cody dressed and went to the diner. A half dozen or so people were in the dining area, and when Cody walked in, they all turned to look at him.

"Good morning, Cody," he heard Lena say. "You staying for breakfast or just tea?"

"I'll have something light with that tea. Got any muffins?" Cody asked.

"Just took some out the oven. Have a seat and I'll bring one over."

The other diners went back to their conversations and Cody sat at one of the rear tables. Lena brought his muffin on a small plate, some butter and honey, and a pot of tea. "Thanks, Lena." He noticed her eyes were red and puffy. "You okay?"

"Not great, but thanks for asking. Need anything else?" she asked.

Cody noticed a slight edge to her voice. Was she beginning to doubt him also, or was it just the series of events in this small town that had her on edge? "Sometime later this morning, if you have a minute, I'd like to ask a few questions. That is, if you're up to it."

"Sure," Lena said. "About nine should work. The breakfast folks will mostly be gone by then."

Since he had a couple of hours before meeting with

Lena, Cody decided to talk to Deputy Freeman. He finished the muffin, drank the last of his tea, and then texted Freeman. "I'm back."

In less than a minute, Freeman replied he wanted to meet and asked if they could meet at Cody's cabin to get away from the prying eyes of the townsfolk. "Sure," Cody texted back.

Before Cody left the dining area, Abe walked in with another man Cody didn't recognize. Abe whispered something to the man who tried to look at Cody without being too obvious.

As Cody walked past them, he said, "Morning, Abe." Then Cody nodded toward the other man and offered his hand. "I'm Cody Hart. Don't believe I've met you."

Abe glared at Cody, while the man mumbled, "Pleasure to meet you," although he didn't look pleased at all. Cody could feel Abe's stare as he walked out. To his surprise, Deputy Freeman was already at the cabin, standing there on the small porch.

"I didn't know you were nearby. Sorry to keep you waiting."

"I was just pulling in when I got your text," Freeman said.

Cody put his key in the new lock Lena had installed and invited Freeman inside. "Have a seat there," he said, pointing to the only upholstered chair.

Cody pulled the wooden chair from the small dining table and sat across from Freeman. "Came back, just like I said I would."

Freeman smiled for the first time since Cody had met him. "I imagine you're putting yourself in my shoes. That about right?"

Cody nodded. "Something like that. What can I do for you this morning?"

Freeman took off his hat and set it on the arm of the chair. "I talked to your commanding officer last night. Nice guy."

Cody nodded. "He is."

"You've got a lot on your mind, it seems. What with your wife up and disappearing. That must be, well, must be a puzzle."

Cody wanted to say something smart but decided that wasn't a good idea. "It's heartbreaking is what it is. I just want to know if she's safe, even if she's with … with someone else."

"I'm sure you being the prime suspect for a while made it even harder. How'd that make you feel?" Freeman asked.

Cody took a deep breath. "Look, deputy, I respect what you do and that you have to question me since I found Tucker's body. But let's just cut to the chase and save us both some time. Am I a suspect?"

Freeman looked at Cody momentarily without speaking, then said, "Nah. You were cleared. In fact, they speak highly of you at the forestry service and hope you'll come back soon. Said you knew those woods, trails, and lakes like nobody else." He cleared his throat. "Sorry for coming on strong. Hard habit to break, you know?"

Cody nodded. "I get it. Is that what you came to tell me, that I'm not a suspect?"

"Well, yes, and that I'd like for you to keep your eyes and ears open. Let me know if you see or hear anything suspicious."

Cody smiled. "I've always wanted to be a spy."

Freeman looked confused. "I don't mean to—"

"Just kidding with you. Of course, I'll let you know. Now I've got something I want to run past you."

Freeman nodded. "Okay."

"Are you now handling the search for Ayita, you know, the girl that went missing?"

"I'm not sure who'll be assigned to Deputy Bowen's cases," Freeman said. "That will be up to the sheriff's office. Unless they find evidence of kidnapping, it'll likely stay in county jurisdiction." He looked down at his feet, then back up at Cody. "Hate to say it, but not much population up here, at least compared to the rest of the state, so it doesn't get a high priority."

"And the fact that she doesn't come from a wealthy family and is Native American, doesn't help either," Cody said.

Freeman cleared his throat. "You said that, not me."

"Any results that you know of from the DNA test on Ayita's backpack?" Cody asked.

Freeman pulled a note pad from his pocket and made a note. "I don't have information on that, but I'll see what I can find out." He rubbed his neck slowly. "But you and I both know DNA results aren't like on TV shows where they get quick answers. The labs are backed up and high-profile cases get priority. Could take weeks, or even longer. You know how it goes. But I'll see what I can find out."

As Freeman disappeared down the narrow path, Cody stayed on the porch, arms crossed. He wanted to believe Freeman was on the level, just a man doing his job. But

Cody had learned over the years that a badge didn't guarantee truth. Sometimes, it just gave a lie more authority.

CHAPTER TWENTY-ONE

Cody heard a tap at the door and got up to answer it. Lena stood there, looking worn from lack of sleep. Sadness lingered in her eyes.

"Come on in," Cody said.

Lena sat in the upholstered chair. "I should get you another chair for this place."

"It's fine. I'm not planning to entertain a crowd." He paused. "How are you holding up?"

Lena shrugged. "I just can't understand why anyone would kill Tucker. He was harmless."

"He seemed like a good guy," Cody said. "How long had you known him?"

"I guess I met him when he first got transferred here." She smiled slightly. "We weren't dating or anything, but we were close. Since we were both outsiders, that gave us a kind of bond." She dabbed at her eyes with a well-used tissue. "He was planning to leave—go back to Charlotte. He wasn't much of a mountain man, as you probably figured out."

Cody remembered the fear in Tucker's eyes when they saw the black bear. "Do you feel up to a few questions?" he asked gently.

Lena nodded.

"Did you know the field was owned by a trust, managed by a trustee down in South Carolina?"

Lena hesitated before answering. "No. But I wouldn't have had any reason to know. Why do you ask?"

"I went to Asheville yesterday to do some research. It just struck me as odd."

Lena tilted her head, studying him. "Are you saying the trust has something to do with Ayita's disappearance?"

Cody realized how strange he must sound. "You know, I'm comfortable in the woods—reading tracks, watching wildlife, all that. But when it comes to tracing ownership and navigating records online? That's not my strength." He looked away. "Nora would've been better at this."

Lena held her hands out, as if appealing to something unseen. "But for whatever reason, you thought finding out who owns that land was important."

Cody ran a hand through his hair. "Yeah. But honestly, I don't know why. As a forestry investigator, I've learned to trust my gut. Sometimes I act on instinct, even when I can't explain it. It drives people crazy. So as odd as it sounds, I just feel like that field matters somehow. I just don't know how—or why."

Unexpectedly, Lena laughed softly and shook her head. "Cody Hart, you are one weird dude."

"Should I be offended?" Cody asked, smiling.

Lena leaned forward. "Just don't go asking Abe these kinds of questions. He's not a fan of yours—in case you hadn't noticed."

"I noticed," Cody said. "Any idea why?"

Lena shrugged. "Maybe it's just because you're an outsider. Around here, that's enough."

She stood. "Is there anything else you need to ask me?

I need to start getting ready for lunch."

"Mira, the lady at the library, said the field was once used for ceremonies. Did you know that?"

Lena swept her arms in a wide arc. "Around here, there's no shortage of legends and folklore." She paused, suddenly serious. "Wait—you're not suggesting Ayita's disappearance was some kind of ritual, are you?"

"I'm not suggesting anything. Just gathering information." Cody then asked, "By the way, what's Sonny's real name?"

Lena shook her head. "Have no idea. Everyone just calls him Sonny."

"When was the last time he was in town?"

"Someone said they saw him around here about a week before Ayita went missing."

Another coincidence?

CHAPTER TWENTY-TWO

Cody was beginning to feel adrift, like he'd lost track of why he'd come to Raven's Rest. Was something going on here? Something more than coincidence?

At this point, he had little else to go on other than gut instinct, that quiet signal that had saved him many times in the forest. He respected it, even when he didn't understand it. And right now, it was telling him there *was* a connection. He just couldn't pin it down yet.

Before heading out, Cody grabbed a protein bar from his backpack and downed it with a glass of milk. Back in New Mexico, Nora would've offered him almond or soy milk. But those options weren't available here. Lena stocked only what sold, just the basics.

Most of the search teams had moved on to other parts of the mountains. Some had disbanded altogether. With no further trace of Ayita, the whispered assumption was that she was no longer in the area, either dead or abducted.

Cody had heard enough of Nora's stories from her work at Aurora Path to know that sometimes death wasn't the worst outcome. The thought of those "what if" possibilities sickened him. He'd seen a few photos of Ayita: dark-haired, small for her age, with an impish smile. His heart ached.

He decided to walk to the field rather than drive. If

anyone questioned why he was there, he could claim he was hiking. But in truth, he was circling around the puzzle in his mind, hoping it might crack open.

When he reached the field, Cody stopped and closed his eyes, trying to imagine the ceremonies Mira had mentioned. Religious rites? Folklore? Ritual sacrifices? Though he was half Navajo, he hadn't spent much time studying his own culture, let alone Cherokee traditions. Still, Nora always said he was one of the most spiritual and intuitive people she knew.

His thoughts drifted to her, as they usually did. Would he ever see her again? Had she died back in New Mexico? If she had simply wanted to leave, why not take her things? Why disappear without a trace? And why, in moments like this, did Cody feel her presence here, like a current in the air? Maybe he was just forcing a connection for his own benefit. He sighed and pushed the thoughts aside. *Focus on Ayita. One thing at a time.*

Midway across the field, he paused. He hadn't seen a single raven. That was odd. He continued toward the tree line, into the woods where he and Tucker had once encountered the black bear. Some folks around town speculated that a bear had taken Ayita. But Cody didn't buy it.

Black bears rarely attacked humans unless they felt threatened, and Ayita knew this area and would have known how to handle an encounter. Besides, she was small, not likely to be perceived as a threat. And there had been no signs of a struggle, no blood, no torn clothing. Nothing.

He moved toward the riverbank where her bracelet had been found. The more he thought about it, the more it felt staged. The clasp had been closed. If someone had yanked it off, it should've been broken or at least unlatched.

And the kayak theory? It didn't hold up. Taking a child in a kayak was risky, and Lena said Ayita had never been in one to her knowledge. That was more of a tourist activity, not for locals, she said. Cody followed the river downstream for nearly half a mile and saw nothing but woods. No cabins. No trails. Just dense forest growing thicker the further he went.

And then he heard it. A soft crack of twigs behind him. He dropped low behind a fallen tree, scanning the woods. Another sound: branches yielding to the weight of something walking. Someone was moving through the forest. Not a bear. A person.

Cody's hand slid to the knife on his belt. It was all he had. Against a rifle, it wouldn't help much, but it was something. He crouched low, steadying his breath. Through the underbrush, he caught a glimpse of a figure: male, not a kid, not an old man. Someone in between.

Then a voice rang out. "Go home, forestry man. You're not welcome here. We take care of our own and don't need you interfering." The figure stepped closer. "This time's a warning. Next time, I'll be a little more clear. Got it?"

Without waiting for a response, the man turned and disappeared deeper into the woods. Cody stayed still, listening, until the sounds faded. Then his phone vibrated in his pocket, startling him. A New Mexico area code. No name, so he let it go to voicemail.

He waited a few minutes longer, then stood from his crouching position and cautiously made his way back toward the field. That's when he saw them. A couple of ravens, pecking at a scrap of notebook paper stuck in the ground with a stake—crudely whittled from a branch. Cody shooed them away. They croaked a harsh, gravelly kraaawk that pierced the stillness. He pulled up the stake and read the message, scrawled in block letters: "One for sorrow, two for fear, three black feathers, and you'll disappear."

The last line, "you'll disappear," was underlined.

CHAPTER TWENTY-THREE

When Cody returned and started up the path to his cabin, Lena was walking towards him, back to the general store. "Hi, were you looking for me?" Cody asked.

"No, not exactly. I saw someone hanging around out here and wondered if they were looking for you."

"Who was it? Do you know?" Cody asked.

"I couldn't tell. He had a hoodie pulled down low, nearly covering his face. It's cool today, but not that cold. It just seemed ... off."

Cody unlocked the cabin door. "Got a minute? I've got something to show you."

"Sure." Lena followed him inside.

Cody pulled the note from his vest pocket. "Someone left me a message."

Lena read it, then looked at Cody. "Where did you get this?"

Cody told her about the note staked to the ground near the riverbank, and the man in the woods who warned him to leave. "So you have no idea who you saw near the cabin?" he asked her.

"Well, I wasn't exactly studying him," Lena said. "But I'd guess it was a man—tall,

fairly young, judging by his gait. Definitely acting secretive. Do you think he's the one who left the note?"

"It's likely. And I'm pretty sure he was driving the

Wrangler that tailed me from the burned cabin." Cody sat on the edge of the bed. "Who's trying to get me to leave town? And why? If they think I'm getting close to something, I wish I knew what it is they think I've figured out."

Lena settled into the chair across from him. "When you told me about going to that burned cabin, I honestly thought you were grasping at straws. But I didn't blame you. If someone I loved was missing and I had any reason at all to think they might be nearby, I'd turn over every rock and search everywhere. Still, I couldn't see how a cabin in the woods had anything to do with your wife disappearing halfway across the country." She stood, pacing a few steps before turning back to face Cody. "You need to tell Deputy Freeman everything." She gave him a small smile. "I'm just getting used to having you around. So don't go and get yourself killed."

Cody looked up at her, struck again by how much she reminded him of Nora—not just in looks, but in spirit. "I'll try not to," he said. "And you're right. I need to come clean with Freeman."

Cody was already in the dining area of the store when Freeman walked in. They had agreed to meet after Freeman's shift. Besides, Lena was making lamb stew, one of Freeman's favorites.

"Hey, man," Freeman said, sliding into the seat across from Cody. "This worked out well. I was planning to stop by anyway. What's up?"

Before Cody could answer, the young woman who often helped Lena came by to take their orders. Once she left, Cody leaned in.

"I need to run a few things by you. Just to get your take."

Freeman raised an eyebrow. "This about Deputy Bowen?"

"I'm not sure, honestly," Cody said. "Let me lay it out, and you tell me."

"Fair enough."

"I came to Raven's Rest because, as you know, my wife Nora went missing in New Mexico over a year ago."

"And you think she came here?" Freeman asked.

Cody pulled a couple of photos from his pocket. "I found these in her belongings. I knew she had relatives in the area, at least at one time, so when the investigation back home went cold, I followed any lead I could, any little scrap. These photos led me to a cabin not far from here. It's partially burned, unoccupied. Lena thinks Abe's family may own it now."

Their food arrived, and they both paused to eat. After a few bites, Freeman asked, "You ask Abe about it?"

Cody gave a dry smile. "We're not exactly chatty. But I found something at that cabin, a green tote bag, the kind Nora used to give the girls she helped through Aurora Path." He explained Nora's work with the foundation and mentioned Baxter Greene, a runaway from this area Nora had been helping.

Freeman listened intently. "And?"

"Greene vanished too. Nora's coworker said she was planning to go on to California. I found a Busbud brochure in the green tote bag at the cabin."

Freeman leaned back. "So you think your wife followed this girl back here, to Raven's Rest? Doesn't make much sense. And even if she did, what's it got to do with Bowen—or Ayita?"

"I know it's thin. That's why I haven't gone to local law enforcement. But I need to tell you that after I left that cabin, someone in a gray Jeep Wrangler followed me. Later, someone ransacked my place and took the tote. There was no forced entry because the door wasn't locked. Lena thought it might be local kids, but this morning she saw someone hanging around the cabin."

Freeman shook his head. "But do you think any of this ties into Tucker's murder or Ayita's disappearance?"

"I don't know. But I was on Tucker's search team briefly. I was with him when we found Ayita's backpack and bracelet. There were drag marks on the bank that made it look like a kayak went into the river."

Freeman squinted. "Made it look like?"

"Yeah. Kayaks leave a specific track, skeg marks and a narrow hull. Definitely not a canoe or raft. I've tracked enough of them to know."

"Thanks for the Kayak 101 lesson," Freeman said. "So someone took her in a kayak. Doesn't help us much."

"Maybe not. There's nowhere to go downriver that I could tell. It's all woods. Dense forest. I think the area was staged to misdirect the search."

Freeman's tone shifted. "I'll have someone check it out. I'm not sold on your theory, but I'll give it some thought. Not even sure who's handling Ayita's case now."

Cody recognized the doubt on Freeman's face. "Look, I'm an investigator, too, and I know this all sounds like a stretch. But these are leads someone should be checking out. As you know, sometimes the smallest detail cracks a case."

He pulled a folded note from his pocket and handed it over. "While I was out there, someone followed me, called to me and suggested I needed to leave town. And then I found this near the river, where Ayita's bracelet was found."

Freeman read the crude message aloud: "One for sorrow, two for fear, three black feathers, and you'll disappear." He pulled out his phone and snapped a photo.

"I think it's time someone talked to Maker," Freeman said.

"Does that mean you're taking Ayita's case?" Cody asked.

Freeman shrugged. "Just saying I'm intrigued."

CHAPTER TWENTY-FOUR

The next day, Freeman went to the town hall, as Cody suggested, and asked around about how he could contact Maker. Only a handful of people were there, and they weren't too cooperative. "Look," Freeman said, "she's not in any trouble. I just need to find out a few things so we can continue the search for …" Freeman couldn't remember the name.

"Ayita," the man offered.

"Yes, sorry, Anita."

"The man rolled his eyes. "No. It's A-y-i-t-a. Pronounced aa-Y IY-Taa."

"Sorry," Freeman said. "No disrespect meant. But I need to talk to Maker. I understand she's Ayita's grandmother," he said, carefully enunciating the girl's name.

The man shifted his gaze to the doorway, where Maker had just entered. "You looking for Maker?" she asked.

The man Freeman had been questioning quietly slipped away when Maker approached the deputy. "Yes, ma'am. May I ask you a few questions about your granddaughter's disappearance?"

Maker nodded. "Over here," she said, pointing to a table and two chairs in the corner of the room.

When Freeman tried to introduce himself, Maker cut him off. "I know who you are. Have you found Ayita?"

"No, ma'am. I'm sorry."

"Are you in charge now?" Maker asked. Her face resembled a mask, showing no emotion at all.

"That hasn't been determined, but I am investigating Deputy Bowen's murder and whether the two events are connected in any way."

Maker nodded slightly. "What do you need to know?"

"You are Ayita's biological grandmother. Is that correct?"

"The Cherokee have a much broader definition of families than some."

Freeman had been taking notes but stopped writing. "What are you saying exactly? Are you biologically related?"

"Family is what you do, who you are. It's more than blood."

Trying to hide his frustration, Freeman continued. "How is it you came to raise Ayita?"

Maker sighed loudly and shook her head. She then mumbled something to herself that Freeman assumed was in Cherokee. "Her mother died. Her father was a drunk. Who else to raise her?"

Freeman cleared his throat. "Ma'am, I'm not here to judge you or to question your good deed in raising this child. But we need as much *factual* information as we can get to continue this investigation."

Maker stared at Freeman, expressionless.

"What about her father?" Freeman asked. "He's called Sonny, right?"

Again, Maker mumbled something to herself that Freeman didn't understand. And then added, "Worthless. That's what he should be called."

"Do you know where we can find him?"

Maker shrugged. "He doesn't live here."

Freeman took a deep breath. "Ma'am, does Sonny have another name?"

"He does, but I never knew his name. He disappeared when Ayita was still in diapers."

"What about Ayita's mother's name. What is it?"

"Ama Ross."

Freeman made a note of the name. "Was Ross her married name?"

"She took on a white name to get jobs. She had lighter hair than most Cherokee, but her name gave her away. So she took on Ross to get work."

"What is her official name? If I try to look up information on her, is she Ama Ross or something else?"

Freeman was startled when Maker grabbed the pen and pad from his hand. "Here, I'll write it down for you. You'd never get it right if I tell you." She scribbled and then handed the pen and pad back to him. "What else do you want to know?"

Freeman closed his pad and put it in his pocket. "Just one more thing. Why would anyone want to kidnap Ayita?"

Again, Maker shrugged. "You'll have to ask whoever took her."

CHAPTER TWENTY-FIVE

Cody searched on his phone for the attorney listed on the trust. Oddly, he was unable to find any information on the law firm, so he began making phone calls.

"Thank you for calling the South Carolina Bar Association," the recording said. It then offered a series of choices for redirecting the call. As instructed, Cody punched the number for a member of the public calling for information. A young woman answered promptly.

"My name is Cody Hart. I'm looking for an attorney named Sterling Ashcroft."

The woman asked Cody a series of questions and then put him on hold. She returned shortly and said there was no attorney named Sterling Ashcroft currently practicing law in South Carolina.

After the call ended, Cody tapped on Freeman's cell number. "Hey," he said when the deputy answered, "I need your help." Cody then asked for Freeman's help with getting more information on Ashcroft.

"Do I need to remind you that you're not on duty here?" Freeman asked. "But just for curiosity's sake, why do you need this information?"

"The field where Ayita's backpack was found is owned by a trust, and the trustee is Sterling Ashcroft. I assumed he was an attorney, but the bar association says he's not a practicing attorney."

"Wait," Freeman said. "Why does it matter who owns the field? It's just open land."

"Well, if that's the case, why the secrecy? You know Raven's Rest. Everybody knows everyone else's business. The general consensus is that Abe's family, who owns most everything around there, also owns the field, but unless Abe has set up this trust, that's not true."

"As I said," Freeman said with a deliberate tone in his voice, "you don't have jurisdiction to go around asking these things. I don't want to get a complaint from someone that you're interfering with an investigation. Leave it to us."

"Fine, I'll find another source. And I'm well aware of my status here, Deputy Freeman."

"Now wait a minute. Just calm down. Let's say *if* I got the information for you, what would you do with it?" Before Cody could answer, Freeman added, "Wait, I don't want to know any more. If by chance *someone* gave you this information, then I don't want to know anything else about it until you can prove there's some relevance to this case. Got it?"

Cody was glad they weren't on FaceTime so Freeman couldn't see Cody's broad smile. "Understood."

Just before the call the ended, Freeman said, "Snapchat," and hung up.

As instructed, Cody downloaded the Snapchat app to his phone. He knew that even if Freeman found anything, it could be days, or longer, before he responded. But within an hour, Cody had a message from Freeman that included an address in Columbia but no phone number.

Cody's gut told him Ashcroft was a key piece of this

puzzle, but even if he had a phone number, he'd rather approach him in person. Cody decided to wait until the next day to take the trip to Columbia, since according to Google, the trip was nearly three hours. He'd need an early start.

CHAPTER TWENTY-SIX

At six o'clock the next day, Lena's dining room had not yet opened. During the early days of the search for Ayita, she had changed her serving hours. But now that the search parties had dwindled or disbanded, she resumed opening at seven. He made a mental note to text her later but then asked himself why he felt he needed to let her know where he was. Maybe it was just a habit from all those years of checking in to let headquarters know where he was and that he was safe.

Nora had been missing for more than a year now, but in Cody's mind, he was just as married as he had ever been. He had always been faithful to Nora, and up until the time she went missing, he had never questioned her faithfulness to him. Lately, he had noticed that he looked forward to seeing Lena but had passed it off as just needing companionship. He had never felt as alone as he had since he left New Mexico. He was a stranger in Raven's Rest, with no connections to anyone. No one except Lena. Perhaps a text to her wasn't a good idea after all.

After driving more than ten miles, he stopped at a service station to get a cup of coffee. Hot tea out here, nearly in the middle of nowhere, would be out of the question. The coffee was hot and strong, but even two small containers of half-and-half didn't dent the dark brew. Cody got a cinnamon bun, which would have to serve as breakfast.

After downing the coffee and the incredibly sweet and gooey bun, he continued on his trip until he eventually reached I-26.

Nearly three hours later, Cody reached downtown Columbia, which was just readying itself for the day. Cody pulled into a gas station on Elmwood Avenue, and after filling his tank went inside to confirm directions to the address. The woman behind the cash register tapped on her phone and then told Cody that Williams-Brice Stadium was less than five miles away.

"Stadium?" Cody asked. "I thought this was a residential area."

"This is Gamecock country, honey. That address belongs to one of the twenty-two cabooses located at Williams-Brice."

"People live in the cabooses?"

"Nah, mostly they're used for parties, corporate meetings, that kind of thing. They're pretty neat." She leaned forward and said in a lower voice, as if sharing a secret, "Wish I had one. But they ain't cheap."

Cody proceeded to Assembly Street toward his destination, to the address Freeman had given him for Sterling Ashcroft. Within a short time, Cody saw Williams-Brice football field.

The cabooses were less than fifty yards from the stadium. Cody parked and walked toward the number he had been given. As he approached the caboose, a woman stopped him. "Can I help you?" she asked.

"Hello, ma'am. I'm looking for Mr. Sterling Ashcroft." Cody began to wonder if he had the right address. "Do you know him?"

"Yes, but he's not here."

"You mean he doesn't live here, or he's just not here now?"

The woman eyed Cody, from top to bottom, and was apparently trying to decide if she could trust him. "Who are you?" she asked. "Show me your driver's license or some kind of identification."

Cody obliged by showing her his New Mexico driver's license and his forestry service credentials.

"You're a long way from home," she said.

Cody nodded. "Yes ma'am, I am. May I ask you a few questions?" When the woman didn't stop him, he took it as a good sign and continued. "He manages a trust that includes some land in North Carolina."

"And what if he does?" the woman asked.

"Are you Mrs. Ashcroft?"

The woman laughed so hard, she started wheezing and pulled an inhaler from her pocket. "No, honey, I do some work for Mr. Ashcroft from time to time, which includes taking care of this caboose," she said pointing to it. "This place is just for meetings, parties on game days, and such. He's a big Gamecock fan and owns several season tickets he shares with clients."

"Is he a practicing attorney?" Cody asked.

She shook her head. "Retired. He comes from money, and rich friends hire him to manage their trusts from time to time."

"I see. I'm here because there's a young girl missing from Raven's Rest, North Carolina. They think she disappeared from a field near town, which is owned by a trust."

"And Sterling is the trustee?" she asked.

Cody nodded.

"If you leave your name and phone number, I'll ask him to call you." She pulled a small notepad and pen from her purse. Cody wrote his name and mobile number and handed it back to her.

"Do you know if Mr. Ashcroft is from North Carolina?"

The woman squared her shoulders. "I can't help you with that. You'll have to ask him."

"Look, I'm not trying to cause any problems, but I drove all morning to see him because I didn't have a phone number. Please don't make me leave empty handed. Can't you at least tell me where his office is?"

She shook her head. "He works from home." She waved toward the caboose. "Or here, or from his car. He's a private man, and he does confidential work. I've been instructed never to give out personal information."

"I understand," Cody said, "and I don't want to get you in trouble." Although he was beginning to question all this secrecy.

The woman smiled and took a step back, signaling the conversation was over. "I'll be sure he gets your contact information. Have a safe trip back to North Carolina."

CHAPTER TWENTY-SEVEN

With no additional information and the sinking feeling that this had been a wasted trip, Cody went back to his pickup and called Lena.

"Where are you?" she asked.

"Columbia." Then added, "South Carolina." He could hear Lena laughing.

"Yes, I'm aware that Columbia is in South Carolina. And it's the capital, or so I hear."

"Sorry, didn't mean to … Anyway, I know you're busy, but do you have any contacts here? I need some information on a retired attorney. Apparently, he's well-heeled, so he may be well-known around here, but the housekeeper at a caboose he owns wouldn't give me anything."

"Caboose?" Lena asked. "Oh, you mean those at the football stadium. I've read several stories about them. Pretty neat. Anyway, I've got a cousin who is an attorney down there. We're not super close these days, but I think she'll help you." She paused. "But first, you need to tell me what this is about if you want me to get her involved."

"Fair enough. The attorney who manages the trust I told you about lives here. I just want to get more information about the beneficiary of that trust."

"But how is knowing who owns that field going to help you find Ayita?"

"To be honest, I'm not sure yet. Just following a lead that may be a dead end. I may be chasing an empty hunch, and if I can talk to Ashcroft, he'll likely tell me I'm wasting my time."

"Well, let me dig up Sam's contact info. Her name is Samatha, but we all call her Sam. She's a smart lady, and I think you'll like her. A bit strong-willed though. Before I give you her contact info, I also want to give her a heads-up. I'll text you her info shortly."

"Thanks, Lena, I—" But she had already hung up.

Cody decided to wait in his truck for Lena's text. Feeling a bit sleepy from the early morning drive, he closed his eyes and leaned back. Suddenly, he could see Nora, smiling with that twinkle in her eyes. She always saw the best in everyone, especially the runaway kids she helped.

His phone vibrated and Nora's mental image vanished. Assuming it was Lena texting him, he was surprised when he saw a New Mexico area code on his phone.

"I'm calling for Cody Hart. Is that you?" the caller asked.

"Yes. Who is this?"

"I'm Detective Fisher. I've recently been assigned to investigate the disappearances of Baxter Greene and Nora Hart. Ms. Hart was your wife, is that correct?"

Cody felt a chill spread throughout his body. "Yes, she *is* my wife." He swallowed hard. "Have you found something?" It was a question he wasn't sure he wanted answered.

"Yes, I'm afraid so," Fisher said.

Cody suddenly felt dizzy. "Did you find …?" He couldn't bring himself to finish.

"We found some remains in the Santa Fe National Forest. Some hikers found a skull and reported it."

Cody could hardly breathe. "Was it … ?"

"No, it wasn't your wife. Dental records confirm it was Baxter Greene."

Cody exhaled with relief. "What was the cause of death?"

"Multiple stab wounds, apparently made by a hunting knife, or at least something with a similar blade," the detective said. "We're working with the forestry service investigators to get game camera footage or anything else that might help us. They suggested we let you know since your wife was working with Greene when she disappeared."

"Thank you. Have you found anything that might help find Nora?"

"No, I'm sorry, we have not at this point. I assure you we are actively working your wife's case. But as you know, her case is cold and there's not much to go on."

"Can you keep me posted on anything else you find? Especially if you find any links to North Carolina."

"North Carolina? Why's that?"

Cody told the detective about the cabin photo and the green tote bag he found there. "May be nothing. May be something," Cody said.

"Did you report your find to New Mexico or the local authorities?"

"What would I have told them? I found a green cloth tote, with no logo or anything to tie it to the Aurora Path Foundation, along with a bus brochure and restaurant receipt?"

"No, I guess not. Just curious though, why didn't the center put their logo on the bags?"

"Nora told me it was because a kid carrying a tote with the center's logo would be like a neon sign flashing 'runaway!' Might make them targets for predators on the street."

"Makes sense," Fisher said. "But were you thinking maybe Greene went back to North Carolina? Because she obviously didn't."

"I'm not sure what any of this means, if anything," Cody said. "I'll hold onto your phone number and let you know if anything develops on my end. And you'll do the same, right?"

After the call ended, Cody suddenly felt tired. The stress of the past year had taxed his emotions. With every little tidbit of information he got, he was hopeful he might see Nora again. But those tidbits were few and far between—and led nowhere. *What happened to you, Nora?*

CHAPTER TWENTY-EIGHT

Not long after the call with Detective Fisher ended, Cody got a text from Lena with Samantha's phone number. Cody replied with a thumbs-up emoji. He took a deep breath to clear his head. Nothing that had happened in the past year made any sense to him. Cody just wanted his old life back, with moments like he and Nora sitting on the porch, reporting to each other on how their day had gone.

Cody's cell phone rang, yanking him back from memories to reality. It was from the number Lena had just texted him. "This is Sam. Lena said you wanted to talk to me."

"Ah, yes, I mean I was just getting ready to—"

"I'm texting you my home address. I'm working here today, not far from where you are if you're still near the stadium."

"Th—" Sam had already ended the call. Cody put the address in his phone's map and started the navigation. After driving a short distance, he was in the section of Columbia that Sam had called Wales Gardens. The address she had given was for a large brick, two-story home with a meticulously manicured yard. A red Mercedes convertible sat in the driveway, just as Sam had said.

Cody sat in the truck for a moment before getting out. The news of Baxter Greene's remains being found was consuming his thoughts. But he had driven more than three hours this morning to get here so he'd better make the most of it. Besides, he didn't know if the young woman's case had anything at all to do with Nora's disappearance.

When Cody walked up the walkway to the black painted door, it opened before he could ring the doorbell, and a woman stood there. "So you had no trouble getting here, I assume." Not waiting for an answer, she motioned for Cody to come inside.

"I assume you're Sam?" Cody asked.

She smiled. "Guilty." She motioned toward the kitchen. "I'm having a cup of coffee. Want one?"

"No, thanks. But water would be great."

"Come on, we'll talk in the sunroom." She walked briskly ahead of Cody. "There," she said pointing to a cluster of chairs. "Sit anywhere you like, and I'll get you a bottle of Pellegrino. Unless you'd rather have tap."

"Pellegrino is fine, thanks." Cody settled down into a wood framed chair with thick cushions, just as Sam returned with the water bottle. "Beautiful neighborhood and house. You lived here long?"

Ignoring his question, Sam said, "Wales Garden is an historic district of Columbia. My parents told me it was built between 1915 and the 1950s. These big old houses are beautiful but a nightmare to maintain."

"I can image the upkeep is pretty steep," Cody said. When Sam didn't reply, he continued, "Thank you for seeing me. Lena says you're cousins?"

Sam stared out the large plate glass window of the sunroom, seemingly watching something in the backyard. "I can't decide if I want to kill them or feed them." She laughed. "Sorry. The squirrels I mean. They eat all the birdseed in the feeders and then demand more. Little buggers." She sighed. "Growing up, Lena was more like a big sister than a cousin, although we're close to the same age. She's a much kinder and gentler person than I am. It's a pity we went our separate ways and lost contact. One needs family, don't you think?"

Before Cody could respond, Sam continued. "She said you want to find someone who is the trustee for some land in North Carolina?"

During his brief exposure to Sam, Cody could agree that Lena was much kinder and gentler, yet Sam was engaging in her own way. He decided not to bore her with the details of how he ended up in Raven's Rest, so he began with Ayita's disappearance. "Yes, Lena may have mentioned to you that a young girl seemingly vanished from a field near Raven's Rest."

"Ah, yes, the infamous field. I went there once when I visited Lena. That place has a lot of stories. Who knows if any of them have any factual basis. But then, that's what makes legends fun, isn't it? I mean, not knowing if any of it is true."

"I'm from New Mexico, and we have our share of legends too. What can you tell me about that field?"

Sam shrugged. "Not much. Just that over the past decade, several women have disappeared from around that area. I don't think any of them were actually from Raven's Rest, and I'm not sure what, if any connection, they had with that field. Like I said, lots of wild stories up there in the mountains. That girl you just mentioned is the youngest I've heard of and the only one from the town itself."

"What do you think happened to those women?"

Sam shrugged again. "Who knows? One can speculate they were taken for some nefarious reason though. And then there's the legend of the ravens having something to do with all of it."

"You mean, like maybe the ravens abducted them?" Cody asked.

"No, silly. I mean like there's talk that an unkindness of ravens shows up in the field before someone disappears."

Cody smiled. "I just recently learned that term, an unkindness of ravens."

Sam laughed. "Isn't that silly? I mean we have herds of sheep, a gaggle of geese, a murder of crows, and so on. When I first heard the term 'an unkindness of ravens' I looked it up. Know where it came from?"

Cody shook his head.

Sam leaned forward, like she was sharing some deep, dark secret. "Well, according to what I read, the term began in the 19th century, because it was believed ravens didn't care about their young. Sometimes, ravens would place their young into the world before they were ready, causing many of them to die. So, some people thought this was cruel, callous behavior. Hence, an unkindness of ravens. Of course, this belief stems from a complete misunderstanding of ravens and nature." She leaned forward, obviously getting into the discussion. "And of course, ravens have a notorious reputation in folklore, thanks in part to Edgar Allan Poe, and have long been associated with dark omens. So perhaps that's where it came from." She leaned back in the chair. "But I digress." She flashed a wide smile. "You obviously didn't come here to talk about ravens." She sipped her coffee. "What does it matter who owns that property?"

"Perhaps it doesn't. But I find it odd that most of the property around Raven's Rest is owned by locals who've been in the area a long time. But this field, full of legends and where Ayita allegedly disappeared, is owned by a private trust. Don't you find that odd?"

"That old guy, I can't remember his name, whose family founded that town. He's a snarky dude. Acted like I was an intruder when I visited Lena."

Cody smiled. "Sounds like Abe."

Sam slapped her palm on her thigh. "Abe. Yes, that's it. His family seems to own everything around there."

"But not that field," Cody said.

"So who is this trustee you're looking for?"

"His name is Sterling Ashcroft. Lena thought maybe—"

Sam interrupted. "Sterling? That's who you're looking for?"

"Do you know him?"

"Like, yeah. I worked for him when I first came to Columbia."

"I went to his caboose, which is very cool by the way, because that's the address on the trust," Cody said. "Luckily, I ran into a woman there who works for him. But she wasn't very helpful."

"God, that woman has worked for him most of her life. She's very protective of Sterling," Sam said.

"Do you know where I can find him?"

Sam stood up and pointed. "That way. He lives one street over."

CHAPTER TWENTY-NINE

Sam tapped on her phone to put it on speaker. Cody could hear it ringing, and then a woman answered. "May I speak to Sterling, please. This is Sam. I'm a former employee and friend."

"I've heard him talk about Sam." The woman laughed. "He speaks highly of you. But I'm sorry, he's not here."

Cody saw Sam roll her eyes. "Have him call me please," and she gave the woman her number.

Sam said to Cody, "He hires that woman to answer his phone when he's busy. Forwards his phone to her. Makes him look more important, I guess. I'll try his home number. He sometimes works there." She scrolled and tapped on the number. When the phone went to voice mail, Sam said, "Sterling, this is Sam. Give me a call. Someone here wants to meet you."

"Sterling makes a living now handling trusts, being a paid estate administrator, and all that stuff," Sam explained. "God, I hope I don't end up like that. Sounds boring as all get out, don't you think?"

Cody shrugged. "Perhaps. Look, I don't want to take up any more of your time. I'll leave my name and cell number with you if you'd please have him call me."

"Of course," Sam said. And then, almost like she was talking to herself, she added. "That is odd that the field is in owned by someone other than the locals. Can't be much value to it. Or maybe it *is* a local."

Cody gave his contact information to Sam and thanked her again for her help. "I'll be leaving now."

"Are you married?" Sam asked.

Startled, Cody wasn't sure how to reply. *Of course I'm married.* But to a woman he hadn't seen in a year and may never see again. "Yes. Why do you ask?"

"Just curious, I guess," Sam said. "You seem a bit, well, lost, for lack of a better word."

Cody smiled slightly. "Yes, that's a good way to describe it." He turned to leave.

"Any reason you can't go down to the Gourmet Shop in Five Points and have a bite of late lunch with me? I'm starving, and I do hate to eat alone."

Cody glanced at his watch. "It's a long drive back to Raven's Rest, so I'd better get going."

"What? And eating a soggy sandwich from a convenience store on the road sounds more appealing to you?"

Cody laughed. "You're pretty direct, aren't you."

"Yes. And I'll drive. No one drives Emily but me." She grabbed some keys from the nearby table. "Emily is my car, of course. A gift from my ex in our divorce settlement."

The Gourmet Shop was a combination food market and small bistro, with both inside and sidewalk tables. Sam led the way and chatted with one of the waitstaff who directed them to a table outside. "Mind if we sit out here?" Sam asked Cody. "I need the fresh air."

"It's fine. I prefer outdoors myself."

"It's also a bit more private. It gets a little cozy inside when they're busy."

They ordered two turkey panini sandwiches and two iced teas. "I'd suggest a glass of wine," Sam said, "but if you're driving a distance, you need to keep your wits about you." Sam pointed to several small birds on the sidewalk. "The little beggars hang out here for bits of bread. I enjoy watching them and sometimes wonder what it would be like to be a bird." She redirected her gaze to Cody. "Do you?"

Cody smiled. "No, I can't say I've ever thought about it."

"This restaurant has been here since 1979. I just read that in an article recently. That's a long time for a restaurant to last. They all seem to go out of business at some point."

The waiter delivered their food and refilled the iced teas. Cody and Sam ate in silence for a few minutes, and then Sam tossed a small piece of bread to the birds, who immediately began fighting over it. "What's your story, Mr. Hart? How on earth did you end up in a god-forsaken place like Raven's Rest?"

Cody took a sip of tea, while considering how to respond. "I think the town is quaint, thought I'd do some hiking there."

Sam threw her head back and laughed. "You are such a bad liar. I'd love to play poker with you sometime." She paused briefly. "Now tell me the truth and what about your wife? Why didn't she come with you?"

Cody shifted in his seat. He was both fascinated with and a bit put off by Sam's directness. "Tell me about yourself first."

"Well, alright. That's fair, I guess. I graduated from law school, joined the Sterling Ashcroft firm, and found out promptly that I hated practicing law. Or at least the kind the firm did. You know, lots of estate work, family disputes over dead people's money. That kind of thing."

"And are you still practicing law?"

"Yes, and I still do some estate work, but I have my own firm now. It's small but it allows me to pick and choose my clients, take off when I want to, and to be myself." She smiled. "And there's my own trust fund, courtesy of my parents, which definitely helps. They also left me the house, which is paid for."

Cody held up his tea glass to toast her. "Good for you. I respect anyone who follows their own path." He took a long sip of tea. "You said you're divorced. Any kids?"

"Goodness no. Can you image me as a mother?" she said laughing. When the waitperson returned, she gave him her American Express card and said, "I know you're busy and you need this table," she said glancing at a line of people waiting for the outside tables, "but I'll leave you a hefty tip if you leave us alone to chat."

The waitperson nodded. "I'll leave the tab but take your time. Let me know if you want refills or need anything."

"Thanks." When he left, she said to Cody. "I can never remember his name, but he's a nice guy. And don't worry, he's used to me, so he won't think I'm pushy." And then added, "Like you probably do."

Cody thought for a moment, trying to decide how he would label Sam if asked. Direct, for sure. But seemingly sincere. "Not at all, but I imagine you're a formidable attorney."

"I can be." She leaned forward slightly. "It's a little-known secret, but I really love my clients and want to help them." She sat up straight again. "I figured as long as I'm doing this tedious work, I might as well help people as much as I can."

The waitperson silently put the credit card and tab on the table and left. Sam scribbled her signature and added a large tip, as promised. "And now, Mr. Hart, you managed to deflect the conversation, but I want to know about you."

Cody hated telling people about Nora's disappearance, because he was never sure he could keep his emotions in check. He pulled up a vision in his memory, of Nora walking along the trail beside him, her hair tossed by the wind. "Nora, that's my wife, disappeared from New Mexico over a year ago."

Sam's hand flew to her mouth. "Oh, no. That's terrible. Is she still missing?"

Cody nodded. "As people say, it's the not-knowing that's so painful." He didn't tell her there were days when he would welcome even bad news if it brought this uncertainty to an end. He went on to tell her about the Aurora Path Foundation, the photo of the now burned cabin, and the green tote bag. And then about Ayita's disappearance and Tucker's murder.

Sam didn't respond immediately. "I'm not sure what

to say. That's a lot to digest. I'm so sorry you're having to deal with all of this." To Cody's surprise, Sam appeared to be on the verge of crying. "Poor Lena. I need to talk to her. She adores that little girl." Sam looked down again at the birds pecking for crumbs. "I wish we had stayed in touch more." She put the napkin from her lap onto the table. "If you'd like, I'll see what I can find out from Sterling. He can be a bit of a … well, you know, a stuffy pain in the ass at times. Is there anything else I can do to help?"

Cody shook his head and glanced at the time on his phone. "I really do need to get on the road, but I appreciate lunch and the offer to help." He smiled. "And if I need a tough-as-nails attorney, I know who to call."

CHAPTER THIRTY

The traffic on I-26 was heavy, and it was late when Cody got back to Raven's Rest. Lena had taped a note to his cabin door telling him she'd be glad to bring him a sandwich if he was hungry when he got home. He removed the note and unlocked the padlock, but before he could get inside, he heard footsteps behind him.

Cody turned around quickly to confront whoever it was. Lena always called his name before approaching, to avoid startling him. This was someone else. The lighting was dim around the cabin, with only a small light on a pole nearly twenty feet away. "Who's there?" Cody called out.

He heard footsteps on the gravel path but no response. As his eyes adjusted to the dark, he recognized the shape of the older woman approaching him. "Maker, is that you?"

"Yes. Do you have a minute?" she asked, still walking toward him.

Cody sighed. "It's been a long day. Could we talk in the morning?"

"It's important, or I wouldn't be here. Let's go inside."

Cody opened the door and held it for Maker. "I left early, so it's a bit of a mess in here, but you can sit there in the chair."

Maker waved his comment away with her hand. "No

problem." Her face, and especially her eyes, reflected sadness.

Cody sat across from her on the edge of the bed, wishing he could just lie down and go to sleep. The drive had tired him, and on the way back, he had found himself thinking of Sam—and then feeling guilty for thinking of another woman. He didn't want to cheat on Nora, but it had been nice to talk to Sam. He liked Lena also, but she was almost too protective at times, like a mother hen.

"What did you want to talk about?" Cody asked.

Maker glanced around the cabin. "Funny, this cabin's been here a long time but I've never been in it. Nice. Lena could make some good money if she rented it to some of those crazy tourists." She made a face, showing her disdain. "But I'm glad she doesn't."

Cody waited for her to get to the point, trying not to show his weariness.

"Lena said you went to Columbia today."

No secrets in small towns. "Yes, I did."

"You've been asking a lot of questions for someone who just came to hike," Maker said.

Cody ran his hand through his hair. He wanted to end this conversation and go to sleep. "I'm an investigator, so it's my nature to ask questions. I'm just trying to find out what happened to Ayita. Just trying to help." He paused to study Maker's face, but she was expressionless. "Why don't you just ask me what you want to know."

"I didn't come to ask you a question," Maker said. "I came to tell you about Ayita."

Cody stiffened. "They found her?"

Maker shook her head. "No. I want to tell you who

she is."

Not in the mood for talking in circles, Cody said, "I understand you're not her biological grandmother."

"She is not my own blood by birth. But in all the ways that matter, she is."

Cody rubbed his neck, trying to stay focused but wishing this conversation would end. "Does this have something to do with her disappearance?"

Maker nodded slightly. "It might. Some people might say I kidnapped her."

Cody stood up from the bed and then he pulled the dining chair closer to Maker and sat. "And did you?"

"Not exactly, but when she was an infant, I took her to protect her from her alcoholic mother, and from Sonny, her worthless sperm provider." She looked into Cody's eyes, her own glistening with tears ready to spill.

In his fatigued state, Cody had not noticed that she had three raven feathers in her hand, which she now held out to him. "I found these on my doorstep the day Ayita went missing. It's from *them.*" Speaking softly, she added, "One for sorrow, two for fear, three black feathers, and you'll disappear."

CHAPTER THIRTY-ONE

Cody examined the feathers Maker handed him, as if touching them might provide some insights. "I guess this is a warning, then."

Maker shook her head. "No, a message."

"What's the message?"

"That the legends are true, the ones about the missing girls."

Cody exhaled deeply to release his frustration. "I'm sorry but this all sounds—"

"Girls have disappeared. You've been asking about the Greene girl, Baxter Greene. Lena told me. That girl went missing from here too. And there have been others over the years, just not from Raven's Rest."

Cody was suddenly exhausted. "Baxter's remains were just found in a national forest in New Mexico."

Maker lowered her head, shaking it slowly from side to side. "I was afraid that would happen."

"My wife, Nora, was helping Baxter. So you need to tell me whatever you know." Cody realized how desperate he sounded. "What's happened to the girls that disappeared? Why were they taken?"

Maker lowered her head. "I don't know. But there are people here in Raven's Rest who do know."

"Who? Cody asked, sounding more demanding than he intended.

Maker lowered her eyes and shook her head.

"Who else knows you took Ayita from her mother?"

"I tried to keep it a secret. But I had to get her away from her old life, the one where she had no future.

"But where is her mother now?" Cody asked.

"Dead, mostly likely. She was a drunk and an addict."

"How did you know her?" Cody asked.

"We both lived in the town of Cherokee and worked for the tourist center." Maker chuckled softly. "Lots of people come to Cherokee on vacation to see *real injuns.* They don't really care much about us or our culture, but we sell them tomahawks made in China at the gift shops." She shook her head. "It's sad, but we made a decent living. But Ayita's mother drank up whatever money she made."

"You said earlier that Sonny was Ayita's biological father but that he left when she was an infant."

Make nodded. "A bum."

Cody studied Maker's face, trying to judge her sincerity. "I think you *do* know Sonny's name. What is it?"

"No, I really don't know." She hesitated briefly. "Sonny wasn't from around here. He came around occasionally to see Ayita, you know, to watch her from a distance, thinking I didn't know about it. But he never talked to her. One day, before she went missing, he asked how she was doing. I told him to get lost. That's the last I saw of him."

"Do you think he took Ayita?"

"No. I dreamed about him right after that. He was falling off the mountain. I think he's dead." She paused. "At least his spirit is dead."

"Have you talked to Abe about any of this?"

Maker's eyes narrowed. "Why would I do that?"

"Well, everyone seems to acknowledge him as the leader of Raven's Rest, whether it's official or not."

Maker shook her head. "I don't." She squinted slightly. "But I do not want him as my enemy either."

Cody rubbed his neck. "Can we talk further about this tomorrow. I'm really exhausted."

"Why did you go to Columbia today? Does it have anything to do with Ayita?" Maker asked.

Cody didn't know whether to scold her for being nosy or how to react. "I don't know at this point." He stood up and walked to the door, opening it for Maker. "We'll talk more tomorrow."

CHAPTER THIRTY-TWO

When his ringing phone woke Cody, he was momentarily disoriented. Looking around the cabin, he remembered where he was and why he was there.

The phone rang one last time before Cody sat up, rubbed his eyes, and looked at the call history. It was Samantha who had called. Tapping on the number, he waited for her to answer.

"Well, someone sure is having a lazy morning," Sam said.

"Sorry, I guess I slept in a bit this morning." He walked over to the kitchen area and put a tea bag in his cup. "Is everything okay? It's early."

"Yes, sorry. I'm an early bird. They get the worm, or so I'm told. Not that I'm fond of worms necessarily. But anyway, I had a long chat with Sterling after you left yesterday afternoon. Thought I'd fill you in if you're awake enough."

"I'm getting there. Go ahead."

"Well, here's the interesting thing. Sterling is the trustee for someone, whom he won't name. He said that was part of the agreement, that he keep their dealings strictly confidential."

Cody poured barely hot water in his cup and dunked the tea bag a few times before dropping it back into the water. "Then you don't really have much to tell me."

"Geez, Cody. I mean, I'm trying to help you. Don't be such a bastard."

Cody laughed. "I haven't been called that since I was back on the job at the forestry service. It was a guy I arrested for hunting illegally, as I recall. And, yes, I know you're trying to help. It's just that I keep hitting brick walls. Did you get anything at all useful from him?"

"Apology accepted, if that was one," Sam said. "And I found out the trust is called Sacred Meadows Trust. I like that, don't you?"

Again, Cody laughed. "Lovely."

"You're making fun, but I just mean that usually a trust is named after the owners, not that it has to be."

"Did he confirm where the land is?" Cody asked.

"He said the trust included several pieces of land near Raven's Rest in North Carolina, and also a significant sum of money and investments."

"Did he elaborate on what he meant by 'significant'?"

"Millions, he said."

"Whew."

"But here's the interesting part. He slipped up and said at one point that a minor was involved. Do you think it could be that child, the one who's missing?"

"What makes you ask that?" Cody asked.

"He sounded worried and said his client would like to talk to you."

"To me? Why?" Cody asked.

"That's all I know. Can you come down here?"

"When? Today?" As much as Cody wanted to get some useful information, he was still bone weary from the long drive.

"No, tomorrow. I've got a guest room here. Why don't you come down and plan to spend the night afterwards. And don't worry. I'll give you all the privacy you want. I'm not trying to be nosy, although that is my nature. I just don't want you to fall asleep behind the wheel and run off the side of the mountain."

Cody pulled the overly steeped tea bag from his cup and dropped it in the small plastic trashcan lined with a white plastic bag. "Alright, I'll be there tomorrow. And thanks for the free lodging."

"Who said it was free?" Sam said laughing. "See you later."

CHAPTER THIRTY-THREE

After the call with Sam, Cody felt ravenously hungry and decided to forgo his protein bar and have a more substantial breakfast. When he walked into the dining area of the store, Lena looked at him and nodded her head toward a table near the back. Maker was sitting there alone.

Cody asked Lena to make him a couple of eggs with toast and then went over to sit with Maker. "Morning," he said. "You're here early."

"Couldn't sleep." She waved her hand toward the front of the store. "Saw that Jeep you've been looking for. Out there, on the street."

"When?" Cody asked. "Just now?"

"No, last night. When I left your cabin. A man was sitting in it, there on the street in front of the store. He was on his phone, so the light from the phone showed his face."

"Did you know who it was?" Cody asked.

Maker shrugged. "Not sure. But I've seen him before. Around town, but not lately."

"Well, let me know if you see him again. I want to know why he was following me."

Maker pulled a slip of paper from her pocket and slid it across the table to Cody. "This might help." She stood up. "I dreamed about Sonny again last night. Maybe he's not dead after all." She nodded to Lena and left the dining room.

Cody picked up the paper and read what Maker had written. He was grinning when Lena brought his food.

"Something funny?" she asked.

"Yeah," Cody said.

Lena put the plate down on the table, shaking her head as she walked away.

Cody stuck the paper in his shirt pocket and finished breakfast. Before he left, he told Lena he'd be out of town again tomorrow and wouldn't return until the following day. "Just keep an eye out, if you don't mind."

"I will. You be careful," Lena said.

When Cody returned to his cabin, he tapped on Deputy Freeman's number in his contacts. After a couple of rings, it went to voicemail. "Hey, buddy," Cody said, "I need a favor. I know you're not supposed to give out this kind of information, but I've got the license plate number of that gray Jeep I mentioned, the one that followed me." Cody pulled the slip of paper from his pocket and read the number. "I'm headed to Columbia tomorrow. Leave me a message with the information. Let's talk soon. I need to fill you in."

Cody decided since he had been telling everyone he was there to hike, that he might actually do some. He really did enjoy a good hike, and it would give him a chance to clear his head. He returned to his cabin and changed into his hiking boots, packed a bottle of water and a few items in his backpack.

Not far into his hike, Cody realized how much he missed being in the forest, walking the trails. It seemed like ages ago since he left New Mexico. His legs felt heavy and stiff, and he found himself breathing harder than he should as he walked up a small incline.

Stopping to take in the scenery, Cody recalled an article he had read about the Blue Ridge Mountains. The name came from their iconic blue haze, caused by the hydrocarbons released by the mountain forests into the atmosphere. The Cherokee were the first to coin the phrase, referring to the mountains as the Shaconage or "land of the blue smoke." He took a deep breath of the crisp, cool air.

Looking around, Cody realized he had walked to the field without making the conscious decision to do so. Maybe there *was* something sacred about this place. Overhead, several ravens circled and then landed on a nearby log. They stared at him, as if waiting for him to move on, out of their territory.

Straight ahead was the place where Ayita's backpack had been found. He went to the spot and kneeled, taking a small handful of dirt in his hand. Who were the people Maker alluded to, the ones who knew what happened to Ayita and the other girls who disappeared? He didn't know Maker well, but he knew enough that pressing her for information would not work. If she had something to tell him, she'd do so when she was ready.

He released the dirt and wiped his hand on his jeans. As he stood up, he heard a vehicle approaching. The path to the field was more of a trail than a road, so it had to be an ATV or something equipped to navigate rough terrain.

Suddenly, a vehicle headed straight for him. The ravens took flight, calling out their familiar kraaawk kraaawk. Cody ran to the tree line and darted between two large trees. The vehicle drove in circles stirring up dust and dirt.

When it stopped, the air cleared and Cody could see that it was the gray Jeep.

As much as Cody wanted to confront the driver, he knew his five-inch hunting knife was no match for a gun or rifle if the man was armed. Cody tried to focus on the driver's face to make out the features, but he had on a baseball cap and sunglasses. When the Jeep didn't leave, Cody decided to walk deeper into the woods, the place where he felt most comfortable, most at home.

He walked along the riverbank and crossed to the other side in a shallow area, stepping from stone to stone, as many others had likely done. When he reached the other side of the river, which was more like a stream at this point, he looked around, scanning the area. Nothing but trees and water.

And then he heard someone approaching from above him on the trail. There's no way the Jeep guy could have gotten here that quickly. Cody rested his hand on the knife, still in its sheath attached to his belt. The person was whistling a tune Cody didn't recognize, and as he came into view, Cody saw a man outfitted with fishing gear.

"Hey, buddy, know any good trout spots around here?" the man asked.

"No, sorry. I'm just out for a hike," Cody said.

"Then you mind if I take a look around here?"

Cody stepped aside as the man approached. "Sure. Come on through. I'm headed on downstream anyway."

"Live around here?" the man asked.

Cody shook his head. "No. What about you?"

"Nah, I'm just an annoying tourist," the man said laughing. We're renting a cabin a little way up the road.

This trip was on my bucket list. I've wanted to fly fish since I saw *A River Runs Through It*, you know that old movie with Brad Pitt?"

"That movie had helped sell a lot of fly-fishing equipment," Cody said, nodding. "Well, good luck. Hope you catch a lot." He took a few steps and turned back. "Mind if I ask you something?"

The man looked up from the gear he had been inspecting. "What's that?"

"Have you seen a man driving a dark gray Jeep Wrangler around here?"

The man squinted. "Yeah, as a matter of fact, I had some words with him just yesterday. He was speeding down the road in front of our cabin, and I was afraid someone would get hurt."

"Did he by any chance give you his name or where he lived?" Cody asked.

"He said his family owned a lot of land around here, and he wasn't aware there were so many tourists around. I didn't believe him, I mean the part about not realizing people were around, but I guess it was nice of him to apologize." The man shrugged. "That's all I know. Sorry."

"Thanks. I'll leave you to your fishing now." As Cody walked up the narrow trail, the man's comments were on his mind. *His family owns a lot of land around here.*

CHAPTER THIRTY-FOUR

The next morning, Cody was on the road, headed back to Columbia to meet with Sterling Ashcroft. They were to meet at 10 am, which meant Cody had to get another early start. The interstate was full of 18-wheelers, as usual, and a dense fog hung low in the air, forcing everyone to slow down.

When Cody arrived at Sam's house, he was a little uneasy about her invitation to stay overnight, but saving more than a hundred on a hotel room helped him get over his uneasiness.

When he pulled into Sam's driveway, he was surprised to see a black Lexus sedan parked behind her Mercedes, probably Ashcroft's. Cody walked to the front door, and Sam was already standing there, with the door partially opened. "Come on in," she said. "We're just catching up since we haven't seen each other for a while. Want coffee? Tea?"

"A cup of strong tea would be nice." Cody stifled a yawn as he followed Sam into the large kitchen and sunroom area, pulling his shoulders back to get the kinks out. Walking for hours was not a problem, but sitting for long periods took a toll on him. "I guess I'm not used to getting up early any longer."

Sam made tea and poured more coffee while Cody and Sterling made small talk about the weather, the traffic on I-26, and other irrelevant topics. Once they had all settled down in the sunroom, Sam broke the ice. "Well, I guess we need to talk about why we're all here. Right?" She smiled at Cody and then Sterling. "Sterling asked to meet with you, Cody, so I'll let him talk. In fact, I'll be happy to leave if you two would rather talk in private."

"I'm fine with you staying," Cody said.

"Same here," Sterling said.

"Then I'll just sit back and let you two talk," Sam said.

Sterling cleared his throat and leaned forward slightly, resting his elbows on his thighs. "Cody, first of all, thank you for driving the distance to be here. We could have talked by phone, I guess, but I wanted you to be able to clearly assess what I'm about to tell you. And that might have been difficult by phone."

"I'm not sure what you're going to say, but face-to-face is usually better," Cody said.

Sterling glanced at Sam before continuing. "Sam told me you have questions about the Sacred Meadows Trust, for which I am the trustee. Also, I am aware that a child went missing from one of the properties in that trust." He shook his head slowly. "So tragic. One can only hope the poor thing is found safe."

"I'm sure you're aware that the odds of finding a missing person diminish greatly after forty-eight hours," Cody said. "And for missing children, the urgency is even greater. Children abducted by strangers are often harmed or killed within the first few hours."

"Yes," Sterling said in a low voice. "I am aware of that, and my client is too."

"Your client, the one who funded the trust?" Cody

asked.

Sterling leaned back and put the tips of his fingers together, tapping them gently. "I know that's your primary question, and I wish I could answer it. But my client wants to remain anonymous."

Cody sat up straight, "But why? What's the big secret?"

Sterling glanced at Sam again, who was sitting silently in a big, upholstered chair with her feet tucked under her. "It's complicated. I wish I could say more, but I am contractually bound to honor their confidentiality."

"But—"

Before Cody could continue, Sterling held up his hand. "Just hear me out. Please."

Cody nodded. "Go on."

"There are several parcels of land my client owns and holds in trust for a single beneficiary."

"Is this land near Raven's Rest?" Cody asked.

"Yes, it is. One parcel is known as 'the field,' which you are familiar with. Another parcel is known as the old campground area, which was acquired from a gentleman who needed some cash—quickly. And there are a few other parcels of land included in the trust also."

"Are the other properties vacant, like these two parcels, or are they developed?"

"All the parcels are undeveloped. That is, if by developed you mean houses, or one of those awful log cabins." Sterling then laughed at himself. "Oh my, what a zinger that was. I don't mean to sound pompous. Not at all, it's just that … well, never mind. I apologize if I offended you."

Since the beginning of their conversation, Cody had tried to place Ashcroft's slight accent. British? It was mixed with a bit of Southern, so it was difficult to tell at times. "No problem. But why did your client buy up land around Raven's Rest? Are they planning to develop it into condos or some kind of tourist thing?"

"Oh, my goodness, no. In fact, that's precisely what the trust was set up to prevent, developing the land around Raven's Rest."

"So your client just expects to hold onto that land and has the money to pay taxes on it forever?" Cody asked.

"Well, as you know, nothing is forever, but my client has the resources to pay taxes for the rest of her … their lifetime, and for the lifetime of the beneficiary."

Cody tried not to react to Sterling's slip-of-the-tongue. So the mysterious client is a woman.

CHAPTER THIRTY-FIVE

It was nearly midday when Sterling Ashcroft announced he needed to leave for another appointment. Holding out his hand to Cody, he said, "I hope you understand the situation I'm in. I wish I could help you, especially since Sam filled me in about your wife. I hope you find her safe."

"Thanks," Cody said. "Please tell your client I would like to meet with … with them. I believe the two cases are somehow linked, so it would be to our mutual benefit to share information and resources. And assure your client I can be as discreet as I need to be." Cody pulled a business card from his pocket and handed it to Sterling. "I'm an investigator on leave from the forestry service, but your client can call this number. They'll vouch for me."

"I'll pass your card and message along. A pleasure meeting you, although I wish it were under more pleasant circumstances." He shifted his focus to Sam and bowed slightly. "Always a pleasure to see you, my dear. Take care and please stay in touch. After all, we're neighbors."

Sam smiled and nodded. "Good to see you too."

After Sterling left, Sam asked, "What would you like for lunch? My treat."

"Some answers, to start with," Cody said.

"Please don't put me in a situation like this. I promised to connect you with Sterling, and I did. That's all the involvement I agreed to. Besides, I honestly don't know who his client is. He's a man of his word if nothing else." She put her hand on Cody's arm. "Come on, I'll make us a sandwich and a cup of soup. And then you can take a nap."

"Sounds good. I'm still a bit weary." Cody's phone vibrated and he glanced at the screen. "I need to go take this. Do you mind?"

"You can go to my office down the hall and shut the door. First door on the right."

Cody tapped on his phone to answer the call as he walked down the hallway. "Hey, you got that tag information for me?"

"Hello to you too. Yes, Cody, I'm fine, thanks." Freeman said sarcastically.

"Sorry, I'm sleepy and hungry. What's up?"

"You were right."

"About what?" Cody asked.

"That I'm not supposed to give you this information. But you being such a charming, thoughtful guy, I decided to make an exception."

Cody laughed. "Now who's being a jerk?"

"Anyway, the tag number is registered to a real estate company in Asheville."

"What's the name of this company?" Cody asked.

"Founders Realty."

"Is that someone's name you think?"

"Not sure."

"I saw him again yesterday." Cody told Freeman about the encounter in the field.

"If you want to file a harassment complaint, just let me know."

"I get the impression he just wants me to leave."

"And what will he do when you don't?" Freeman asked.

"Thanks for cheering me up. And I really do appreciate your help. I'm in Columbia, but I'll be back tomorrow and will fill you in on a few things."

Cody returned to the kitchen where Sam was ladling soup into large mugs. "Go ahead and have a seat. I've got the sandwiches ready. Iced tea okay?"

"Sounds good," Cody said.

During lunch they talked about Columbia, Raven's Rest, and New Mexico. When they ran out of small talk, Sam asked, "Do you think your wife is still alive?"

Startled by her directness, Cody stammered, "I … I'm not—"

"I'm sorry, that was an insensitive question," Sam said. "I didn't mean to make you uncomfortable. It's just that I can't imagine what you must be going through, what you're thinking."

"It's like a nightmare I can't wake up from."

"If you don't want to talk about it, we can go back to talking about the other forty-seven states in the union."

Cody laughed. "We were having a pretty superficial conversation, weren't we?"

Sam smiled. "Superficial but interesting." She paused. "Do you want to talk about her, about Nora? I might be impertinent, but I am a good listener."

Cody wasn't sure whether he *wanted* to talk about Nora, but he *needed* to talk to someone. Being in Raven's Rest without family or friends had been more difficult than he imagined. "Nora and I were opposites in many ways.

But also alike in many ways. We were best friends, as corny as that sounds." Cody ran his hand through his hair. "Funny thing is, she begged me to get into a different line of work. She was afraid I'd get killed out in the woods chasing poachers or drug dealers." He put his face in his hands and then looked up again. "And then she goes missing. All she ever wanted to do was to help those kids."

"Are you sure her disappearance has something to do with her work?" Sam asked.

Cody sat back in his chair, looked at the ceiling and then refocused on Sam. "No. I'm not sure of anything at this point. There are times I wonder if she just needed a change. But there's no indication that's what happened. And if she didn't leave voluntarily, then someone took her."

"I guess they checked all the hospitals and … and the morgue?"

Cody nodded. "I can't fault their investigation. They did a thorough search." He sighed. "That's what drove me to Raven's Rest, grasping at anything, no matter how small the connection might be. And I guess I just needed to get away from … from our home, the places we went together." He cleared his throat. "So here I am in Columbia, tracking down a trust for a missing girl, which may or may not have any remote connection to Nora." He smiled. "Sounds pretty pathetic when you think about it."

Sam cocked her head slightly. "And yet, the investigator part of you feels there *is* some connection."

Cody stood. "Look, I need to get back to Raven's Rest." When Sam started to speak, he held up his hand to silence her. "It's nothing you said or did. You're a gracious host, and I'm very grateful for all you're doing to help. But that call gave me some information I need to check out. And as much as I'd like to relax and hang out with you, I need to get going."

Sam stood up and took his hands in hers. "I get it. I really do. Just promise me that when all this is behind you, and if you should find yourself alone ..." She smiled. "Come back to see me."

CHAPTER THIRTY-SIX

Before leaving Columbia, Cody stopped to get a large cup of Starbucks coffee. Not because he particularly liked it, but he knew it would keep him awake on the more than three hours' drive ahead.

By the time he reached Raven's Rest, it was dark and the sky warned of an approaching storm. The general store was closed and dark, but as he walked up the path to his cabin, he saw a small light. Was it inside the cabin? He couldn't tell.

As he approached, he realized the light was from a propane lantern on his front porch. It was sitting on the small table beside the rocking chair. And someone was sitting in it, although he couldn't see who it was.

"Hello, who's there?" Cody called out. "Who are you?"

"I had another dream," a voice called out.

"Maker, is that you?" Cody asked.

"Who else you talking to about dreams?" Maker said, chuckling.

Cody got the key from his pocket and removed the padlock on the door. He walked in first and then motioned for Maker to follow him. "What did I do to deserve another late-night visit from you?"

"Guess it's your lucky day. And if you'd stay home sometime, I wouldn't have to sit here waiting on you."

"Well, I had actually planned to return tomorrow. Would you have sat here all night?" Cody threw his backpack on the unmade bed.

"I read somewhere that making your bed each morning teaches you that little things in life matter. And if you can't do the little things, you'll never accomplish the big things."

Cody laughed. "So I guess you never fail to make up your bed."

Maker shrugged. "Sometimes I do, sometimes I don't." Her smile disappeared. "Ayita always made hers and reminded me that little things matter." She shook her head slowly. "I sure miss her."

The expression on Maker's face signaled she needed a friend right now, not a lecture about unexpected visits. "So you said outside that you had another dream. About Sonny?"

Maker shook her head. "No, about Ayita. She's okay—for now at least."

"Look, I sure hope so, but …"

"You think I'm a silly old woman, and I am. But I've been living life longer than you, so that makes me a little smarter, in some ways. And even though you're part Navajo, that part has been civilized right out of you. You've forgotten the old ways." She made a grunting noise. "If your mother ever taught you."

"My mother tried, but you're right. I've forgotten a lot of what she tried to teach me." Cody sighed. "Want a cup of tea before you tell me about that dream?"

Maker shook her head. "Nah. I got to get my beauty rest. Tea will keep me awake." She looked around the room. "Nice place. Are you going to stay here for long?" She held up her hand. "And don't give me that 'I'm just here to hike' crap."

Ignoring her question, Cody said, "So tell me about that dream."

Maker sighed. "Last night, in a dream, Ayita talked to me. She said we were wasting time looking for her in the woods."

"By any chance did she tell you where we *should* look?" Cody asked.

"Be patient, will you? I'm getting to all that." Maker rubbed her hand, and Cody noticed for the first time the arthritic gnarls in her fingers. Considering how much she worked with her hands, it wasn't surprising. But he was surprised he had not noticed until now. Perhaps he was getting rusty. As an investigator, he had been attuned to every detail, no matter how minor. *The little things are important. Pay attention.*

Maker continued. "In my dream, Ayita reminded me I had taught her how to survive in the woods. And how to live peacefully with the bears and other wildlife. But she said she wasn't allowed outside, so I shouldn't worry the bears had gotten her."

While Cody wasn't sure how credible Maker's dreams were, he wasn't ready to dismiss them either. "Is she in the mountains?"

Maker shrugged. "She just told me to feed the ravens."

"What does that mean?" Cody asked.

"Ayita feeds the ravens in the field every day. She loves that land. It's sacred, you know. Or at least that's the legend." She looked up at Cody, meeting his gaze. "It's sacred because of the virgins who were taken from there. Their pure spirits make it sacred."

Feeling numb with fatigue, Cody asked, "Exactly how many other girls have gone missing from around here?"

"Only two from close by, at least since I've been here." She paused. "But others have gone missing, from nearby places, or so I've heard."

"Look, I need to get some rest, and you need your beauty sleep. But was there anything else in your dream that might help us find her?" Cody asked.

"Only that she said I should trust you." Maker stood to leave, and then added, "And she hopes you find your wife."

Stunned, Cody asked, "But how does she know about Nora? I've never talked to Ayita."

Maker shrugged and then walked out into the night.

CHAPTER THIRTY-SEVEN

When Cody got up the next morning, he had a raging headache. His body ached from driving more than six hours yesterday. And he kept waking up thinking about Maker's comments. Was she a wise woman—or just trying to get him to continue searching for Ayita?

Since Lena was watching out for the cabin, he needed to let her know he was back from Columbia and was now headed to Asheville to talk to the owner of the gray Jeep that kept following him. But when he walked into the diner, her part-time help waited on him, saying Lena had taken the day off. She assured Cody that Lena was fine, just taking a break to do some errands.

Cody finished his breakfast and put a few things in his backpack. As he walked down the path to his truck, he saw Abe standing there, waiting for him. "Morning, Abe."

Abe didn't respond. "You know, I'm trying to give you the benefit of the doubt, but I haven't seen you hike much since you've been here."

Cody stared at Abe. "So you came over to my cabin, early in the morning, to let me know I need to improve my exercise program? Is that it?" Cody could feel himself getting angry. "The last time I checked, my activities are none of your business. Or did I miss the memo that says otherwise?"

Abe took a step forward. "You watch that mouth,

mister. This is *my* town, so anything happening here *is* my business." He shifted his gaze to Cody's backpack hanging to one side. "You taking another road trip?"

Cody managed to smile. "Nah, just going to do some hiking. Thought I'd try some trails near Asheville. I hear the folks are a lot more welcoming there." He brushed past Abe, intentionally bumping him with the backpack. "You have a nice day now."

When Cody got into his pickup, Abe left. What was that all about? Did Abe know Cody had been to Columbia? Had someone followed him? Or reported on his whereabouts?

Pushing the questions aside, Cody focused on his plan for the day and what he would say to the driver of the gray Jeep.

Several times, when Cody checked his rearview mirror, he saw the same car behind him. He wasn't sure how long the car had been there and had no reason to be concerned, at least at this point. After all, there were only a few main roads, and most likely the car behind was headed to Asheville also. Besides, he reminded himself, he had been following the same car in front of him for miles himself.

By the time Cody reached Asheville, traffic had thickened. The city had earned its reputation as one of the fastest-growing in the country, and it showed—mountain views, endless restaurants, and crowds to match. Even after last year's storm, downtown hummed with life, its fresh paint and bustling sidewalks proof of a town that knew how to endure.

He saw his destination, Founders Realty, on the other side of the busy street and drove several blocks until he found a parking lot with a few empty spaces. After parking, he took a few deep breaths and reminded himself to stay calm. After all, he had no real proof that anyone at the real estate company had been following him.

After walking a few minutes, the real estate company was in view. It had a large plate glass window facing the street, and Cody could see a man and woman inside. Before going in, he decided to walk down the narrow driveway beside the building to the small parking area behind it.

Since it was still early, only a handful of cars were parked: a silver Lexus, a black Kia SUV, and a gray Jeep Wrangler. Cody recognized the tag number as the one Maker had scribbled on the scrap of paper.

As Cody turned to walk back to the sidewalk, the back door of the real estate building opened and a man stepped outside. "Looking for something?"

Cody walked forward and extended his hand. "Morning." The man ignored his handshake offer. "Matter of fact, I am looking for something. The owner of that gray Wrangler. Know who that might be?"

What business is it of yours?"

"You the owner?" Cody asked.

The man turned to go back inside. "Get lost or I'll call the police."

"I think that's a good idea. I'd like to tell them about a gray Jeep with this tag number that's been following me. I'd call that stalking, which as I recall, is against the law here or anywhere else."

The man took a step toward Cody. "This is a free country, in case you hadn't noticed. I can drive anywhere I want without your permission, Mr. Hotshot Forestry Investigator."

"Ah, so you do know who I am." Cody held up his hand. "Just getting my phone from my pocket, so don't get jittery."

The man's shoulders tensed. "Just leave, okay?"

"Not until I get some answers." Cody pretended to tap his phone's screen and then said, "I'd like to report a stalking."

The man stiffened again and walked to within inches of Cody, punching his chest with his finger. "You don't know who you're messing with, man. Go back to New Mexico. Ain't nothing here you need to worry about." He then brushed past Cody and got in the Jeep, spraying dust and gravel as he sped away.

Cody walked back to the front of the real estate office and looked inside. As far as he could tell, the woman was the only person there. "Hi, ma'am," Cody said as he walked in.

"Hello, how can I help you?" she asked.

"Is the owner here? Someone in town told me he was good to work with."

"He was here, but you just missed him. I saw him leave just a moment ago."

Indeed you did. "Maybe you can help me," Cody said.

"Of course. Are you looking to buy or rent?" she asked.

"I'd like to make a note of the owner's name, so I

could talk with him later."

"Sure. His name is Skip, at least that's what everyone calls him."

"Is that Skip Founders?"

The woman laughed. "Oh, no. Founders is just the name of the company. It's Skip Corbett."

"Was Skip's family the founding family of Asheville? Is that where he came up with the name?" Cody tried to show sincerity.

"No, but they did establish a small town that's northwest of here, Raven's Rest."

"Ah, interesting. I'll have to check that out," Cody said.

She shrugged. "Not much there, if you ask me. Lots of mountains, trees. And bears, of course," she said smiling.

Cody was glancing around the office when he caught sight of a photograph. "Is that the Santa Fe National Forest?"

The woman glanced at the framed photo hanging on the wall. "Yes, I believe it is. Skip visited the area about a year ago and came back raving about how beautiful it was. Best trout fishing anywhere, he said. In fact, he plans to develop some land up near Raven's Rest that his family owns, you know, a luxury fishing resort." She looked back at Cody. "Have you ever been to New Mexico?"

"You might say that." He turned to leave. "I'll check back later when Skip's here. Thanks."

CHAPTER THIRTY-EIGHT

Cody decided to explore Asheville a bit before heading back to Raven's Rest. Mostly because the city was teeming with all kinds of people: seniors, teenagers, throwback hippies in tie-dye tees and torn jeans, and all the Gens—X, Y, and Z. In contrast to the sleepy atmosphere of Raven's Rest, Asheville energized him.

He stopped in a quaint but touristy store and bought a few postcards. He had no one to send them to, but maybe one day, when he was back in New Mexico, he could show the postcards to Nora and tell her about his search for her. Maybe they could even laugh about it.

As Cody was leaving the shop, a man stepped into his path. "Excuse me—Cody Hart?"

Cody stopped short. "Yes. Do I know you?"

The man extended a calloused hand. "I'm Everett Rawlins. Most folks call me Sonny."

Cody hesitated before shaking his hand. "Okay. So how do you know who I am?"

"Word travels." Sonny shifted awkwardly. "A buddy of mine lives in Weaverville and has been helping with the search. He's doing some electrical work in the building across from Founders Realty. He met you at the search and called me when he saw you arguing with Skip."

Cody's eyes narrowed. "You have people keeping tabs on Skip?"

"Not exactly. He's just a friend who doesn't like

what's going on up there. And he knows I've been trying to keep an eye on the search as best as I can, from a distance."

"And you're Ayita's father," Cody said.

Sonny nodded slowly. "Not much of one, I'll admit. But yeah. I just wanted a chance to talk to you."

Cody scanned the street. "This isn't the best place. There's a lot just up the block where I parked. We can talk there."

"I'll follow you, a little way back," Sonny said.

Cody nodded and walked away, feeling Sonny's presence not far behind.

When Cody returned to the parking lot, he stood beside his pickup, waiting for Sonny, who walked up a few minutes later.

Based on what Maker had told him, Cody assumed Sonny would look more like a typical drunk. But instead, his hair was neatly cut, and he was tanned and fit, like someone who spent a lot of time outdoors.

"Mind if we sit in your truck?" Sonny asked. "You can pat me down if it'll make you more comfortable, but I haven't owned a gun or any other weapon since I hunted with my pop as a teenager."

Cody unlocked the truck and got in the driver's seat. Sonny got in and closed his door. "Well, I have to say you're the last person I expected to see today," Cody said. He studied Sonny's face, hoping to pick up on something that would signal whether he could be trusted. "Do you know where Ayita is?"

Sonny leaned back against the headrest. "No, man, I swear I didn't have anything to do with it." He turned slightly in his seat so he was nearly facing Cody.

"Do you know who might have taken her?"

"No, just some suspicions," Sonny said.

Cody was beginning to feel uncomfortable sitting in the parking lot. While Sonny seemed safe enough, Cody's senses were now on high alert.

Despite Maker's denials, Cody now suspected she stayed in touch with Sonny, even though she claimed he was still an unfit father and a drunk. "You and Maker stay in touch?" Cody asked.

Sonny looked out the window and surveyed the surroundings before responding. "I see her sometimes. You know, just to ask about Ayita." Sonny laughed softly. "She doesn't like me much, but I guess you figured that out."

"That's the impression I got. Look, how about we continue this over lunch," Cody said. "I'm starting to get a little hungry. Any place not too far away but far enough?"

Sonny nodded. "We can head over to West Asheville. I know a little place there."

Cody drove while Sonny gave him instructions. Eventually, they ended up at a mom-and-pop diner next to a small hardware shop that looked like something out of the fifties. "Don't worry, the food's good," Sonny said. "Almost as good as Lena's."

Inside, an older man nodded at Sonny and motioned toward a booth near the back of the dining room. As soon as they were seated, the man came over. "Want your usual?" he asked Sonny, who nodded affirmatively. "And what about you?" the man asked Cody.

"What do you recommend?" Cody asked.

The man laughed softly and pointed to Sonny. "What

he's having."

"Fine," Cody said. "I love surprises." When they were alone again, Cody said, "You're obviously a regular."

Sonny shrugged. "I work for a landscaping company not far from here, so I come here often."

Their meals were served quickly, which turned out to be meatloaf, mashed potatoes, and lima beans, served with a basket of cornbread. During the first few bites, they ate in silence.

"How's your meal?" Sonny asked.

"Not bad. Back home, I'd likely be having black beans and rice, so this is not so different. Besides, Southern cuisine is starting to grow on me." Cody took another sip of tea. "I take it you know Lena?"

Sonny nodded. "She's a good woman. It's a shame about her husband."

Cody realized he knew very little about Lena's past. "How's that?" he asked Sonny.

"Drunk driver killed him years back. Broke her heart. That's why she moved to Raven's Rest, you know, for a new start."

"You seem to know her pretty well." Cody asked.

Sonny shook his head. "Nah, nothing like that. But people talk, you know?"

"So tell me, what do you know about your daughter's disappearance?" Cody asked. "And what about her biological mother. Could she be involved?"

"That's not likely. I heard Ama, her mother, died years ago."

Cody could see the pain in Sonny's expression. "What happened?"

"She was a drunk, and then she became an addict. I loved that woman with all my heart, but I couldn't help her. Eventually, she pulled me down into her hellhole and I began drinking. A lot."

"I'm sorry for your loss."

Sonny shrugged. "She never forgave me for letting them take Ayita away." He looked away briefly, pain etched in his face. "But I wasn't in the picture much at that point."

Cody recalled his conversation with Maker in which she admitted to taking Ayita from her mother and Sonny. "You agreed to let Maker take her?"

Sonny lowered his head and nodded. "Maker promised to raise like her own grandchild. Besides, that beautiful baby girl deserved more of a life than me or Ama could give her."

"I'm sure that was hard for you."

"Didn't have a choice if I wanted Ayita to have a decent life. If Child Protection had taken her, no telling where my baby girl would have ended up. I couldn't bear the thought of losing her forever, maybe never seeing her again." Sonny wiped his eyes with the back of his hand. "Sorry, man. Didn't mean to get all emotional like."

Cody was mentally piecing together all the tidbits he had learned from Sonny, but nothing provided the answers he needed. "So you don't know anything about who could have taken Ayita? Or why?"

Sonny sat up straight and pulled his shoulders back. "I want to hire you to get her back."

From his conversations with Maker, Cody was under the impression Sonny was a bum and a drunk. "I don't mean to be rude, but I thought you were destitute."

Sonny smiled briefly. "I was, believe me, for many years. But I got myself together with the help of this church center down the road. Once I got straightened out, they got me a job with that landscaper. So I fixed myself up, got clean clothes, and a decent place to stay."

"You seem as good as most dads I know. Why didn't you go back and get Ayita once you cleaned yourself up?"

Sonny glanced around the dining room of the small restaurant, suddenly looking uncomfortable. "Ayita is much better off with Maker. What do I know about kids?" He looked up at Cody, eyes brimming with tears. "Ever had a small, helpless baby hold onto your finger like you're the most important person in the world?" Without waiting for a reply, Sonny continued. "It's like nothing else, man. Truth is, I was scared. I'm clean now, but what if … Once you're an alcoholic … well, it's a lifetime sentence."

Sonny took a long drink of iced tea, then wiped the condensation off the side of his glass with a napkin. "There's something you need to know. Ayita has a large trust fund that will be hers when she's eighteen."

"You talking about the trust that owns the field and the old campground?"

Sonny nodded. "I think there's cash money in that trust too, or so I heard."

"Are you looking to cash in on all that money?" Cody asked.

Sonny leaned forward and made eye contact with Cody. "No, man. I mean, no. I would never …"

"Relax, I believe you. *For now, at least.* What else do you know about that trust?" Cody asked.

"Not much, just that Ama's sister, Wesa, felt sorry for Ayita, because her mother had OD'd, and I was a hopeless drunk during those days. Wesa told me to stay away from Ayita and let Maker care for her until Ayita turns eighteen, when she'll get the trust fund and decide her own life. I knew I couldn't give Ayita anything close to that, so I stayed out of her life." Sonny shifted in his seat. "And Wesa told me she would revoke the trust fund if I ever tried to claim Ayita."

"But you were a different person then," Cody said. "I'm sure she'd be happy to have you in Ayita's life now."

"If I wanted to be a father, you know like on a daily basis, I might have fought back. But there's a fine line between being sober and waking up not knowing where you are or how much you drank. I can't risk it, so this arrangement works for me. And for Ayita. Can you understand that?"

"No, I honestly can't, but it's not my place to question you or the aunt."

"At the time her name was Wesa, it means—"

"It means cat," Cody said, "like an animal that's clever and independent. It's a Cherokee name."

Sonny smiled. "I thought you looked a little Cherokee, what with that dark hair and those brown eyes."

"Navajo, actually, but only half. Got a few Cherokee buddies at the forestry service."

The owner appeared at their table to offer drink refills, which both men declined. "Today's special is on the house." He put his hand on Sonny's shoulder. "Always good to see you, my friend."

Cody smiled as the man left. "He must really like you.

Thanks for lunch."

Sonny shrugged, "I do some free yard work for him from time to time."

"Let's get out of here," Cody said. "We've probably overstayed our welcome."

The two men walked out to the parking lot together and shook hands. "Good to meet you, Sonny," Cody said. "Where can I drop you?"

"No need. I'll get a ride back to my car from one of the other workers."

"If I need to get in touch with you, is that number you called me on good?" Cody asked.

Sonny nodded. "What I said earlier, about wanting to hire you, that's for real. Heard you're a hot shot investigator."

Cody realized his past life now seemed like someone else's—someone who had a wife, a solid career, and few cares in the world. But that was then. "Searching for Ayita is about all I've done since I got to Raven's Rest. No need to hire me, I'll keep looking." Cody kicked at a large chunk of gravel in the parking lot. "You say you don't know who took Ayita, but you've got suspicions. Mind telling what you think?"

Sonny shrugged. "And I need to ask why you're so interested in finding her."

"I've got my reasons," Cody said. "Besides, from what I can tell, she was a great kid. I hope she's alive and well." Cody glanced around the parking area, looking for the gray Jeep. "By the way, you mentioned that Wesa was the aunt's name at the time. Did she change it?"

Sonny shrugged. "I think so, but I don't know what

name she goes by now. Don't even know her married name. It's not like we're pen pals or anything." He paused and looked around the parking lot. "But I do know the land in Ayita's trust is worth a small fortune. Developers have been trying to get it for years, especially that field."

"I heard there's some talk about it being sacred."

Sonny nodded. "Ayita could feel it. I could tell when I watched her dance and feed the ravens."

"What about that old campground. I heard that was now part of the trust too."

"Yeah, so I heard."

"I also heard you used to own that land. That true?" Cody asked.

Sonny smiled. "Nah, man. I haven't ever owned that land. I think Abe's family did a long time ago. Heard he sold it to Wesa to raise some cash." He rubbed his neck. "But that's just talk. I don't keep up with all that."

"Anybody you know who's waiting to snatch that land?"

Sonny nodded. "I think you talked to him today."

CHAPTER THIRTY-NINE

On the drive back to Raven's Rest, Cody had left a message for Deputy Freeman, asking if he was free to meet him at the diner. Cody wanted to fill him in on his conversations with Skip and Sonny. But he was now nearly in town and hadn't heard from Freeman.

Bone tired and hungry, Cody decided to see if Lena had anything he could eat. A bowl of stew or soup would be great, but he'd take a cold sandwich if that's all there was.

He walked toward his cabin to drop off his backpack first. A noise, Cody wasn't sure what, caught his attention. Perhaps it was a deer or a raccoon. With his senses on full alert now, Cody continued walking slowly until he got to the cabin door. As he reached in his pocket for his key, someone pulled a dark cloth bag over his head. It smelled of animals and dust. "What the …" Cody struggled to get lose, but realized there were four arms, not two, restraining him.

"Be still and listen," a gruff male voice said.

Not struggling was more of a challenge for Cody than trying to get away, as all his senses and years of training urged him to fight back. "Who are you? What do you want?"

One set of arms was obviously stronger than the other, and the stronger set shoved Cody against the door of the cabin. "You don't belong here. Go home and let us take care of our own." Another hard shove. "Got that?"

"And what if I like it here?" Cody asked, knowing he'd provoke another shove. But he wanted to keep the man talking and was mentally recording the characteristics of the voice. Had he heard it before? The man seemed to be intentionally altering his voice, which meant he was afraid Cody would recognize him.

"Then you're a dead man," the other man said. While not as strong as the first voice, the second voice was older and more menacing. "And you can join your sweet wife in paradise."

Cody felt the bile rising in his throat. "What did you—" But before he could finish, he was hit with something hard and fell to the ground.

"Cody! Wake up, Cody!" The female voice sounded far away, yet he could feel someone's presence. "We need to get you to a hospital."

And then Cody felt something very cold on his forehead. He tried to sit up.

"Whoa there. You lie still."

Lena? Was she his attacker? No, she couldn't be. Cody was confused and had a raging throb in his head. "What …"

"Just be still. Can you open your eyes and look at me?" she asked.

Cody slowly opened his eyes, trying to focus on her face. Right now, she looked like an angel with auburn hair.

"What happened?" he asked.

She held up two fingers together. "Follow my fingers."

Cody pushed through the raging pain and tried to focus on her slim fingers as she moved them slowly from side to side.

"What is your name?"

Why is she asking that? "Cody," he said.

"And where are you?"

"Right here. With you," Cody said.

"I think you may have a concussion. And you've got one helluva knot popping up. If I help you, can you get inside?"

Cody tried to get up unassisted but couldn't. "Maybe," he said.

After a few trials and errors, Lena found a way to support him while he got up. Somehow they managed to get inside the cabin and stumbled toward Cody's bed. He fell onto it when he tried to sit down.

For the next few minutes, Lena fussed over him, checking again to be sure nothing was broken or bleeding. "I think you're okay, but I'd like to drive you over to Urgent Care in the next town, just to be sure."

Cody again tried to focus. "I've had worse, but thanks."

"Do you feel like telling me what happened? Did you fall? I need to get better lighting for that path."

Cody managed to reach out and take her hand. "Enough with the mother hen stuff. I'm fine." When he realized he was still holding her hand, he squeezed it slightly and then released it.

"I was bringing you some chicken noodle soup I made today, but when I saw you on the ground, I set it down outside. I'll go get it and warm it up."

"I've always heard chicken soup will fix anything," Cody said, managing a slight smile. He relaxed into the soft down pillow and was almost asleep when Lena started shaking him. "Don't go to sleep. You're supposed to stay awake after a concussion."

Cody managed a weak smile. "That's not medically accurate, but I promise not to slip off into paradise." Suddenly, his body tensed. Why had he said that word—paradise? And then he remembered what the guy said and his smile vanished. "Did you see anyone when you came up?" He tried to sit up, and finally with Lena's assistance, he was able to prop the pillow against the headboard and lean against it.

"No, I didn't. Sorry. Did someone attack you?"

Cody tried to remember. "I think it was two men. They came up from behind and put a cloth bag of some kind over my head, so I didn't see their faces. One was older, one younger and stronger."

"Did you recognize their voices?"

Even if Cody had, he would not have admitted it to Lena. Not yet. Once he had his focus back, he needed to replay the recording in his memory and try to zero in on any phrases they used. And why 'paradise'? He didn't recall Nora ever saying anything about paradise. Vaguely, he remembered watching the 1984 movie "Footloose" on TV with her one night. She had been captivated by one of the songs, "Almost Paradise," and had walked around the house singing it for days. For a brief moment, Cody basked in the memory of Nora's often off-key rendition of the love song.

"Cody, are you alright?" Lena asked.

The memory slipped away. "Yeah, sorry."

Lena put a tray on his lap and he ate the soup like it was a magic elixir that would erase the last year of pain. "Delicious," he managed to say. "Thanks for taking care of me."

Sitting in a chair beside his bed, Lena leaned back and put her hands on her hips. "Looks like you need someone to protect you. We need to call—. Oh, I almost forgot, Deputy Freeman texted me when he couldn't reach you. Said you had left him a message."

Cody handed the tray to Lena. "Ask him if he can get over here tonight. I need to talk to him."

CHAPTER FORTY

More than an hour later, Deputy Freeman arrived at Cody's cabin. Lena greeted him and then left the two men alone to talk.

"Pardon me for saying so, but you look like crap," Freeman said to Cody.

Cody grimaced as he tried to reposition himself. "You should see me from my side." He then tried to move again so he could face Freeman. "Ouch."

Freeman looked at Cody's head. "That's a pretty good goose egg you got there. Looks painful."

Cody moved his head more slowly this time. "Yeah, it hurts."

Freeman settled into the chair Lena had just vacated. "I take it you didn't walk into the door or do anything self-inflicted. Is that why you wanted to see me, to file a complaint against someone?"

"If I knew who attacked me, I would, but I didn't see either of them."

"Them? More than one?"

Cody gave Freeman the scant details he could recall.

"So you have no idea who did this?" Freeman asked.

"Let's just say I have my suspicions, but no, I don't have enough to be sure."

Freeman glanced around the cabin. "I'd love to have a place like this, up a little further on the mountain with no one close by."

"My idea of a getaway has changed a good bit since I got here. Let's just say this ain't paradise." *That word again. Why did it keep popping up*? Lately, his memories of Nora had become a two-edged sword: pain and pleasure.

Cody continued, "I wanted to tell you about my meeting with Skip Corbett. And then about my meeting with Sonny, Ayita's father."

Freeman pointed at Cody's head. "You see. This is what happens when you start poking around in police business."

Cody reminded himself not to overreact. "First of all, I am still an investigator with the New Mexico Forestry Service, so I'm not a stranger to police business. And frankly, I don't think Ayita's disappearance is getting the attention it deserves. Is it because she's indigenous?"

Freeman held up his hands in mock surrender. "Whoa there, Mr. Investigator. I'm not the bad guy here. Who else would drive to this place at this hour to listen to a guy telling me I'm not doing my job?"

Cody pushed two pillows against the wall and leaned back. "Sorry. You're right. My head is throbbing, and I'm upset with myself for letting those two thugs surprise me. I must be losing my edge."

"I get it. No harm done. Tell me about Ayita's dad first." He paused. "And for your information, the lack of attention to her case isn't about her lineage. We're just short-handed, and this place is somewhat remote, which doesn't help. We searched everywhere, and I do mean everywhere. There's no trace of her, which is unusual, to say the least. With no sign of struggle or abduction, it's like …

well, almost like she just went off willingly with someone."

"I hope, but doubt, you're right. Anyway, Sonny works for a landscaper in West Asheville." Cody reached into his pocket and pulled out a crumpled business card. "Got this from him in case you need to talk to him."

Freeman studied the card. "Considering you didn't have much to go on, I'm impressed you found him."

Cody smiled slightly. "I should just take that compliment and run with it, but he found me. He approached me on the street after I paid a visit to Skip's real estate office."

Freeman put Sonny's business card in his pocket. "I figured after you got that owner info from the tag number, you'd be paying Mister Gray Jeep a visit."

Cody smiled. "Oh, so while you're telling me not to get involved, you also know I'll do some of your work for you. You're using me. Is that about it?"

"I'm just an overworked deputy working a case that makes no sense. So, yeah, I appreciate your insights and your help," Freeman said, smiling. "And for the record, you're enjoying the challenge. I think you miss work—a lot. So stop complaining." Freeman sat back in the chair. "Did you learn anything from Sonny? Are you convinced he's not involved?"

"Well, he tried to hire me to find his daughter. I mean, that could have been to throw me off track, but I don't think so. He's a recovering alcoholic, just trying to hold his life together." Cody paused briefly. "There is something though. Sonny told me Ayita's aunt set up a trust fund to take care of Ayita, her sister's child. And the aunt warned Sonny that if he tried to regain custody of Ayita, she would revoke the trust fund. He's okay with that since he doesn't want to play daddy, although I got the impression he'd do anything for that kid."

"Who's this aunt?"

"Well, here's the thing. Sonny only knows her by her Cherokee name, Wesa. He thinks she goes by another name now. He hasn't talked to her in years, since just after Ayita was born. Apparently Wesa is well off and runs in different circles now."

"Send me all this information when you feel like it, and I'll see what I can find out. Since you couldn't get this attorney in Columbia to tell you, I may have to get a judge to order the release of that information. And without any solid evidence that the trust is in any way involved in Ayita's disappearance, it's unlikely a judge will approve it." Freeman shrugged. "But we'll see. And what about Skip? You think Skip's involved?"

"Absolutely, but I'm not sure how or how deep. I accused him of stalking me. Maybe I just don't like the guy." Cody decided to withhold, for now, seeing the photo of New Mexico at the real estate office. He was afraid if he connected those dots, the image might be even more terrifying than he imagined. And that's all it was right now, just a bunch of unconnected dots.

CHAPTER FORTY-ONE

The next morning, Cody awoke with a raging headache and wondered if he should have let Lena take him to urgent care last night. He sat up slowly, checking his vision by focusing on various objects around the cabin. Everything came into focus—except the answers to his questions.

He stayed in the shower longer than usual, as the warm water was soothing to his aching body. Had he not heard his phone ring, he would have stayed in even longer. In his weakened state, he didn't want to rush out and risk falling, so he got out of the shower slowly.

By the time he was able to check his phone, he saw a voicemail from an unknown number. He wasn't familiar with that area code and had no idea where the caller was from. Cody was about to call back when he heard a faint knock on the door. After last night, he wasn't taking chances. "Who is it?" he called out.

"Lena sent me. I have a tray for you."

"Let me throw on some clothes." He quickly grabbed some jeans and a wrinkled shirt. When he opened the door, Lena's part-time assistant was standing there with the tray.

"Thanks," he said. "That was nice of Lena. And of you, of course, for delivering it." He felt a little embarrassed at all the attention.

Setting the tray on the small dining table, Cody decided a hot meal trumped his curiosity of finding out who called him. The food was good and made him realize how hungry he was. As he was taking the last bite of homemade sourdough toast and jam, his phone rang again. The screen showed the same number from the voicemail left earlier.

Cody wiped his mouth with the napkin from the tray. "Hello?" Since there was a brief silence, he thought it might be a prank call or wrong number. "Hello," he repeated.

"Is this Cody Hart?" a female voice asked.

"Yes. Who's this?"

"I … you said you wanted to talk to me," she said.

"And who are you?"

"Katherine, but most people call me Kat."

Even in his weakened state, Cody's mind made the connection instantly. The Cherokee name Wesa means cat. Now this woman named Kat calls. Too much of a coincidence, as Abe would remind him. "What can I do for you, Wesa?" he asked.

"I … how did you …?" She sighed loudly. "Sterling said you were clever. Yes, I am, rather I was Wesa. I had my name legally changed years ago. What few Cherokee relatives I have left still use Wesa, but all my friends call me Kat."

"Obviously, I have a lot of questions for you, but I'd rather not do this over the phone," Cody said. "I'd offer to drive to Columbia, but I had a small accident last night, and I'm just not up to a long drive. Perhaps—"

Kat interrupted. "The reason I called you back is because I wanted to ask if you could meet with me closer up your way. Are you up to driving to Asheville? I think that's fairly close to you. If not, we can meet another day. I really don't want to be seen in Raven's Rest."

"I can make that drive. It's only about an hour from here."

"I can be there by eleven. Does that work with your schedule?"

"I'll make it work. Where in Asheville would you like to meet?" Cody asked.

"Are you familiar with the Grove Park Inn?"

"No, but I'll find it," Cody said.

"I'll text you the address. There's a wonderful lunch restaurant there."

Cody left a message for Lena on his dining table, knowing that if he didn't return, she'd check the cabin. In his prior life, he would never have worried about these things. But now, he had reason to be more cautious. Someone had made him a target.

Cody pulled up to the historic inn just before eleven. Inside the grand lobby of the Grove Park Inn, he took in the quiet elegance—polished wood, stone hearths, and the low murmur of conversation. The place had a kind of quiet dignity that reflected its history.

A hotel employee approached and directed him to the front desk. "I'm not here to check in," Cody said. "I'm just meeting someone."

"Yes, we were anticipating your arrival. The front desk will direct you to your companion," the hotel employee said before nodding slightly and walking away.

Cody approached the front desk, "I'm—"

"Mr. Hart, welcome to Grove Park Inn. Your lunch guest is seated. I'll take you to her."

Cody followed the woman to the restaurant and then to a table. "It's a bit chilly and windy out, so we've set you up inside," the woman said. "I hope that's okay."

"Of course," Cody said.

The woman motioned toward a woman sitting alone at a table, gazing out a window with a gorgeous view of the mountains in the distance.

Kat called out to Cody, motioning for him to join her. "Please," she said, "have a seat." When Cody was seated, she held out her hand. "I'm Kat, and it's a pleasure to meet you. May I call you Cody?"

"Of course. Nice to meet you too," Cody said.

Kat focused on the knot on his head. "That's a nasty bump. I hope you've been checked out properly."

Cody nodded, not wanting another person fussing over him. As soon as he was seated, a waitperson arrived at the table to take their order. Kat made a suggestion, which Cody agreed to. "You've obviously been here before," Cody said. "And frequently, by the treatment you get. You must tip well."

Kat laughed softly. "You're always looking for clues, aren't you?" She lowered her voice. "It's a nice discreet place to meet. And the food is delicious." After taking a sip of iced tea, she added, "Maker and I meet here sometimes."

Cody wasn't sure he heard her correctly. "Maker?"

"That's not her real name, of course, but that's the

name you and everyone else in Raven's Rest know her by."

Cody leaned back in his chair. "So you two stay in touch. Are you close friends?"

"Let's enjoy our lunch and then we can talk freely," Kat said. "They'll let us stay, uninterrupted, as long as we'd like."

Cody managed to withhold any further questions until after they had finished eating, but the swirl of unconnected dots was dancing in his head again. He wasn't aware Maker and Ayita's aunt were in regular contact. But considering all he'd learned, he wasn't totally surprised either.

"I asked them to bring us a pot of tea with our dessert. Maker says that's your preference. Correct?"

Cody nodded as he studied Kat's features, hoping they might give him insights into this mysterious woman. She had black hair with slight graying around the temples. Her dark eyes were mesmerizing. When Cody made direct eye contact, she held his gaze without hesitation, as if she was used to people staring into her eyes. She reminded Cody of his mother.

"I'm sure you have a lot of questions," Kat said. "And I'll try to answer them." She poured each of them a cup of steaming tea. "Shall I just start from the beginning?"

"Please do."

Kat gently put her cup back on its sauce and stared out the window briefly, as if gathering her thoughts. "As you know, Ayita's mother, Ama, and I were sisters. She was nearly five years younger. After our mother died of pneumonia, I was only seventeen, and we were on our own. In many ways, I became Ama's mother."

Kat looked out the window. "Raising Ama was a challenge. She wasn't a strong person and eventually gave in easily to alcohol and later to drugs." Kat shook her head and looked away briefly. "And then to various men who took advantage of her. I tried to help her, but she didn't want to be helped." Kat dabbed at her eyes with an embroidered handkerchief; a genteel item Cody had not seen in many years. "When Ama met Sonny, I thought he might be able to save her from herself. But instead, she took him to hell with her." She paused. "Sorry, I guess part of me is still angry with her for not being here for Ayita. You know what that's like, don't you?"

Cody nodded, unable to find the words to reply. There were days he was so angry with Nora for being gone. But mostly he was angry at life itself for taking her away from him.

"When Ama died, I accepted responsibility for Ayita's future," Kat said. "It was the least I could do. But I never wanted to be a mother."

Cody recalled Sonny's declaration that he didn't want to be a father. Poor Ayita. No one wanted her.

"So that's why you asked Maker to raise her," Cody said. "And why you set up the trust for Ayita."

Kat nodded. "The trust came later, but yes, I did. I'm an executive for a large international firm, and I've been blessed with a substantial income." She smiled slightly. "And I have a wonderful investment advisor who has made me what some would call wealthy. My husband, God rest his soul, died of cancer several years ago and left me a substantial inheritance." She cleared her throat to regain her composure. "But the trust fund is not just about money for Ayita and providing for her needs, her future. It's also about preserving the field and other land around Raven's Rest. Ayita loves that field and goes there every day to feed those ravens she loves so much."

Cody remembered Sonny saying the same thing, and that he used to watch her dance in the field. "Who are you protecting the land from? Abe's family?"

"Yes, but there are others too. As open land becomes more scarce, developers are like vultures, scavenging the area for scenic property to develop."

"So from what you've told me, Ayita is rich, or will be when she's eighteen," Cody said.

"Yes, she is well provided for and won't have to sell any of that land to live comfortably. She's the only beneficiary of the trust, my only heir."

Cody exhaled deeply. "I'm sorry I haven't been successful in finding Ayita."

Kat gently put her hand on Cody's. "And I'm sorry for your troubles. But I wanted you to know we're grateful for all you're doing to find Ayita." She paused and took a deep breath. "But you need to stop."

"I can't stop being sorry for not finding her, but I—"

Kat patted his hand again. "No, Cody. I mean you have to stop looking for Ayita."

CHAPTER FORTY-TWO

Between Cody's headache and Kat's strange request, he was having trouble making sense of it all. "I'm sorry, I guess I'm not following you. Why would you want me to stop?"

Kat looked off into space momentarily before she refocused on Cody. "I'm sorry for the intrigue. I'm not trying to be mysterious, but there's so much you don't know."

"I've got the time to listen if you've got the time to tell me," Cody said.

Kat took a deep breath and looked at him with those deep, dark eyes. "As you know, Ayita's trust contains, among other assets, several parcels of land near Raven's Rest."

"Did you buy the land from Abe or his family? I was under the impression they owned most of the land around the area."

"That's mostly true—or it was. Over the years, the Corbett family sold off pieces to pay taxes and other expenses. But the field, the one where Ayita's backpack was found, has always been in our family. Back when my mother owned it, it had no real estate value. Now, Abe and that crooked nephew of his want it—and they'll do anything to get it."

"I met Skip yesterday. It was more of a confrontation

than a conversation. Are you suggesting he had something to do with Ayita's disappearance?"

"No, Cody. I *know* he did," Kat said, her voice hardening. "They're holding Ayita for ransom. They want me to sell them the field and the old campground at a ridiculously low price." Kat paused to look out the window. "Or they'll sell her."

Cody stiffened. "Sell her? To who?"

Kat nodded. "I have no doubt they're serious. There have been whispers for years, rumors that the Corbett family is involved in trafficking. No proof. No witnesses. Just girls who vanish and families who eventually stop asking questions."

"Why haven't you gone to the authorities?"

Kat's expression hardened, her chin protruding slightly. "Do you think I haven't tried? Years ago, I reported suspicious activity anonymously and nothing happened. Then someone followed me home. A week later, my tires were slashed in my company's garage. That was their message: 'We know who you are and we see you.' I got scared. And not just for me."

Cody stared at her, waiting.

"You don't understand, Cody. The Corbetts aren't just some backwoods clan. They can influence judges, deputies, maybe even feds. Abe's brother was mayor once. His cousin sits on the board of a private bank in Asheville. Even if I could get Skip and Abe arrested, there are more of them. People you'd never suspect. And if I stir the waters too much, Ayita will …" She shook her head slowly.

Cody ran a hand through his hair. "Do you really think they'd sell her?"

"Yes. They'd sell her, like inventory. The same way they likely sold the others. It's why I can't risk going public. She'll be gone, and I'll never find her."

"Jesus," Cody said. "Are you going to give them the land?"

Kat hesitated. "That land is sacred. My great-grandfather held ceremonies there. My mother took me there to pray. I tried to take Ama there, to heal her. But she laughed at me."

"Maker told me she took Ayita from her mother," Cody said. "But it was you."

Kat nodded. "Ama and Maker both worked in Cherokee at one point. That's where I met Maker. She saw what was happening to Ayita and begged me to take her myself. But I couldn't raise a child—didn't want to. My career was taking off, and I traveled constantly. So I made arrangements for Maker to take her. But Maker didn't want to leave the area, so she began visiting nearby towns, close enough to stay in the mountains she loved but far enough away from Ama. On one visit, Maker met Lena and told her she was raising a grandchild alone and wondered if it would be a good place for them to move to. Lena assured her the town was safe."

"Did Ama ever look for Ayita?"

"Not that I know of. She died of an overdose not long after Maker and Ayita left town. I don't think she ever really cared about that child." Kat's voice cracked. "But I failed Ayita too. I thought setting up a trust for her would make things right, for her and for Maker. Instead, I put Ayita in more danger. If anything happens to her… it's on me."

Cody's tone softened. "You thought you were doing the right thing. But why shut Sonny out of Ayita's life? He's turned his life around, but he said you threatened to revoke the trust if he contacted Ayita."

Kat sighed. "It sounds so cold when you say it like that. But I'm not sure he is her biological father. Ama had … other men. But even if he is, Sonny was drinking heavily then, and I didn't trust him to be a good parent. Still don't, although I give him credit for trying to make a better life for himself."

Cody leaned in. "So you want me to stop looking for Ayita, but you haven't said what you're going to do."

"I don't know," she said. "If I give them the land, Ayita might return. If I don't ... then she disappears."

Cody exhaled slowly. "Do you know why I came to Raven's Rest?"

"Maker said you thought your wife might be there."

He smiled. "That makes it sound so simple, but it's not. Nora worked at the Aurora Path Foundation in New Mexico and was working with a runaway girl named Baxter Greene. She was from an area near Raven's Rest. A few days ago, Baxter's body turned up in the Santa Fe National Forest, near our home. My wife's case has gone cold as ice, and I still have no idea where she is."

Cody looked down at his hands as he clenched them, fingers intertwined. "When I found a photo of a cabin outside of Raven's Rest, I came here to look for Nora, mostly out of desperation because I didn't know what else to do. When I found the cabin, which is half burned now, I also found evidence that possibly ties the Aurora Center to it." Cody paused, composing himself.

"Maker says it may have been a holding location for their enterprise," Kat said. "I've heard such rumors myself."

"And Deputy Tucker Bowen, who was looking for Ayita, he's dead," Cody said. "Murdered. They found his body at the old campground, the land your trust owns." He rubbed his eyes. "So you see, this isn't just about Ayita anymore. I'm not going home. Not until I know what happened to Nora. Not until I find Ayita. And if I can bring down the Corbetts while I'm at it, all the better."

Kat's tears spilled over. "While I hope it's not true, it's possible your wife was killed somewhere between New Mexico and Raven's Rest." She paused, looking out the window again. "Or brought here to be sold."

CHAPTER FORTY-THREE

For a brief moment, the restaurant, Kat, the people, everything in Cody's universe was spinning out of control. Kat had just voiced his worst fear, making it real. And it felt like a punch to the gut.

He heard Kat's voice, but it sounded far away. "Cody, are you alright? Cody?"

He managed to regain control. "Yes, I'm … I'm sorry."

"I didn't mean to upset you. I shouldn't have been so blunt, and I pray I'm wrong."

It was unimaginable to Cody that his sweet, innocent Nora had been killed and discarded somewhere along a highway between New Mexico and North Carolina. Or might even be buried near Raven's Rest. Yet, they had come across the country to kill one of Nora's runaway teens, dumping her body in the forest Cody used to roam daily.

Even more unthinkable was that Nora had been brought to North Carolina and sold. It was like a knife in Cody's soul. Hearing another person echo Cody's deepest fears was unbearable. Nora sold? By Abe and his nephew? But why? After all, she was in her mid-thirties, older than the typical trafficking victim. Still, Cody also knew from his own cases in New Mexico that older women, and sometimes men, were taken and sold for domestic help, as slaves basically, in faraway countries. Were Abe and Skip so intent on punishing Nora for helping Baxter Greene that they wanted to punish her? Or did she confront them? Too many questions—too few answers.

As if she had heard Cody's thoughts, Kat continued. "I'm afraid while your wife was working with Baxter, she may have discovered something incriminating against the Corbett family." Kat studied Cody's face. "That family is capable of anything, I'm afraid."

"But Nora would have told me if she had reason to be afraid," Cody said. *Or would she?* Perhaps she only had suspicions and kept them to herself so he wouldn't worry. The local authorities had questioned Nora's manager and co-workers extensively but nothing had pointed them in the direction of the Corbett family.

Feeling his anger rising inappropriately toward Kat, because she was the only person there, he said, "Nora wasn't some pampered heiress playing rescue games. She dedicated her life to helping kids who had nothing. And no one else to turn to." He felt his anger—and his sorrow—rising. "So stop with the riddles and secrets." Cody wiped his eyes with his napkin. "I'm sorry. I don't mean to take any of this out on you."

Kat met his gaze and held it briefly. "I understand."

"Why do you think Deputy Tucker Bowen was killed?" Cody asked. "Do you think he learned the truth? Or saw something at the campground?"

Kat stared out the window for a moment. "We may never know, but I've heard that the old campground is supposedly an exchange location."

"What do you mean by that?" Cody asked.

"Where the exchanges are made. The rumors are that the girls are sold online and then delivered in the old campground to a transporter who takes them to a private airfield somewhere nearby." Kat sighed and shook her head. "But that's all speculation."

Cody massaged his neck, trying to relieve the tension. "If everyone is talking about all this, why has the whole town remained silent? I don't get it."

"Sadly, I'm afraid there's probably a devil's agreement in place. Abe's family or whoever is snatching these girls agreed not to take the locals as long as they keep quiet."

Cody's mind was swirling, trying to grasp all Kat was telling him. "But they took Ayita, and she's local." Before Kat could answer, Cody realized the answer was obvious. "But she's a rich little local girl."

Kat nodded slowly. "Yes, she is."

Cody tried desperately to collect his thoughts. If what Kat said was true, the rules of this place, of this whole investigation, had just changed.

CHAPTER FORTY-FOUR

On the drive back to Raven's Rest, Cody's thoughts bounced around in his head. Was it possible that Abe or someone nearby was holding Nora? Was she alive? Or was he just desperately creating hope where there was none?

By the time he got to Raven's Rest, it was getting dark. The lights were still on in the general store, so he went inside and was glad to see Lena was working tonight. How much was she aware of what was going on? Had he been totally wrong to trust her?

"Hi there, stranger," Lena said. "I've got a bowl of rice and cowboy beans I saved for you if you'd like it."

"Sorry, I'm not hungry. But a cold beer would be great," Cody said.

"Coming up." Lena left for the kitchen and returned with beer in her hand and a bowl of peanuts and pretzels. "In case you want something to munch on." She sat down across from him. "You look tired."

Cody wanted to blurt out his feelings but refrained. "Just a lot on my mind. I need to talk to Maker."

"Odd that you'd say that," Lena said. "We've all been looking for her. She hasn't been in and no one seems to have seen her in the last two days."

"Is that unusual?" Cody asked.

"Very. She usually comes here at least once a day. Or she'll stop in the Town Hall and chat with a few people."

"Have you told Deputy Freeman?" Cody asked, his shoulders tensing.

"Well, no. I mean …"

"Has anyone checked her cabin?" Cody asked.

"I was planning on going over there myself. Hoping you might go with me." Lena studied Cody. "But if you're too tired, I can go alone."

Cody sighed. "I'm just tired of all the drama in this little town." He looked into Lena's eyes. "And the secrets."

When Cody and Lena got to Maker's cottage, the front door was partially open. Lena looked at Cody and her hand flew to her mouth. "This doesn't look good."

Cody reached into his backpack and pulled out his hunting knife. "Maker?" he called out. He looked around the room, which had been tossed. He had no idea what might have been taken, if anything. "We need to call Freeman. I'll check all the rooms and then look around outside. Go sit in the truck and wait," he said pointing outside, as if talking to a child. "And lock the doors." Lena dutifully followed his instructions.

Cody searched the rooms and then stepped outside. The cabin was built on a concrete foundation, so there was no crawlspace. An unlocked storage shed was behind the house and contained only a few gardening tools and an old weaving frame in need of repair.

Walking back toward his truck, Cody tapped on Freeman's number in his contacts. "Hey, buddy, I need to report a missing person. Call me when you get this, no matter what time."

Lena was sitting in the truck, looking wild-eyed and scared. He knew he had to either trust her and let her know what he'd found out or cut her out of the conversation completely. Perhaps because he was tired, worried, or on the verge of giving up, he decided he needed a friend.

He got in the pickup and said to Lena, "I'll take you back to the store and then I need to wait for Freeman to call back."

"I'll wait—" she began.

"No, I don't want to worry about you." Cody smiled slightly. "I've got enough on my plate to worry about. I promise to fill you in on what I've found out. But in the morning. I'm just about done in for today." When Lena started to speak again, he held up his hand. "No, just … let's not argue. I'm tired."

After he dropped Lena off at the general store, his phone rang and Freeman's number appeared. "Hey, buddy, what's up?"

"I'm not sure where to start. First, has anyone reported Maker missing?"

"No, why?"

"She hasn't been seen for days, which is unusual. Lena and I went to her cabin. It's been tossed, but I don't know if it was a break-in or something else." Cody felt wearier than he could ever remember.

"I can meet you at her cabin, but I need for someone local to file the report," Freeman said. "No offense, man, but you're just a visitor there."

"Understood. Can Lena do it?"

"I suppose. Are there any relatives? Or what about

Abe? He seems to be the go-to guy in Raven's Rest."

"No," Cody said more emphatically than he intended. "Don't talk to him just yet. I'll meet you at the general store and give Lena a heads-up that you're coming by."

Freeman laughed softly. "I'll say this. You know how to stir up a town."

CHAPTER FORTY-FIVE

When Cody arrived at the general store, he was relieved to see the lights were still on in the kitchen area. He wasn't keen on the idea of having to wake Lena up to file a missing persons report on Maker.

He knocked on the back door that led directly into the kitchen area but got no reply. He knocked again, this time harder. "Lena," he called out. "It's me, Cody." He continued knocking until the door opened.

"Geez, Cody, I hear you," Lena said. "Come in."

Cody looked around the area behind the building before going in. "Lock the door," he said.

"Should I make some fresh coffee?" Lena asked.

Cody nodded. "Freeman is coming over to talk to us. Might be a long night."

Lena held up a finger in acknowledgment. "Plenty of coffee. Got it."

Cody sat at the table and was nearly asleep when Lena appeared with two steaming cups. "You want anything to go with this?"

Cody smiled slightly. "Yeah, a few days of sleep, somewhere as far away from here as I can get." Before Lena could respond, Freeman texted to say he was at the door.

After letting Freeman in, Lena poured more coffee for Cody and got a mug for Freeman. Freeman looked at Cody. "Well, you called this meeting. What's going on?"

The weight of all that had happened settled on Cody, nearly overwhelming him. "As I said, Maker seems to be missing." Cody looked at Lena. "You need to file a missing persons report, since I'm just 'a visitor,'" he said looking at Freeman.

"But do we really know she's missing?" Lena asked.

"I think when I tell you what I've found out, you'll agree there's reason to think so," Cody said.

Freeman leaned back in his chair and pulled out a small notebook from his pocket. "Alright then, go ahead."

Lena gave the deputy all the information she had, which wasn't much. "We should bring Abe into this conversation," she said.

"Before you do that, I need to fill both of you in on my meeting with Ayita's aunt." Cody had promised Kat not to go to the authorities, but he had no choice now with Maker missing. Too much was at stake: Ayita and Maker—and maybe Nora. For the next twenty minutes, Cody told them about his conversations with Skip and Sonny. He then told them he had met with Ayita's aunt, Wesa, who now goes by the name Kat.

At this point, both Freeman and Lena were staring at him like he had lost his mind. "There's more," Cody said. "I think someone from this area abducted Nora also." Cody told them about Baxter Greene's body being discovered in the Santa Fe National Forest, about the picture of New Mexico in Skip's real estate office, and about Sonny's suspicions.

"What is Kat's take on all that's happened?" Lena asked.

Cody sighed and took another long swallow of coffee. "Ayita is not just some little kid. She's trust-fund rich and is being held for ransom in exchange for the land in her trust."

Freeman ran his hand through his hair. "Man, if I didn't know you better, I'd swear you were loco." He shook his head slowly. "And you think Abe and his nephew are involved?"

"I can't be sure whether Abe is actively involved with his nephew's enterprise, but I'd bet money on it. As I've been told since I got here, Abe knows everything that goes on." Cody shrugged. "Perhaps he just looked the other way, but I doubt it."

Freeman made a few more notes. "I'll get this report filed right away, and we'll put out a missing person's report on Maker."

Lena was looking worried and confused when she spoke. "This is all too much for me to take in." She looked at Freeman. "Is there still an active search for Ayita?"

"We've searched everywhere, on foot, on horseback, by ATV. As far as we can tell, whoever took her went by water."

"To throw off the canine search," Cody added.

"That's my bet," Freeman said. "We're still doing what we can to look for her, but the trail is cold." He tapped a finger on his notebook. "But this new information may lead us to her." He glanced at Cody. "Any perhaps others. But, as you know, the first forty-eight hours are critical. After that … well, the odds drop significantly."

Lena put her hand on Cody's arm. "And what about

Nora? Are they still looking for her in New Mexico?"

"The investigation has gone stone cold, but officially they're still looking." Cody shrugged. "There are some folks who still believe she left voluntarily."

Freeman stood up to leave. "I need to get the ball rolling on this. Send me the contact info on Ayita's aunt. If she's aware of a kidnapping and didn't report it, she could be in big trouble." He pointed his finger at Cody. "Good job on all this, but back off now. Let us handle it. These people, whoever they are, are dangerous. Got it?"

CHAPTER FORTY-SIX

Cody had difficulty getting out of bed the next morning. It was as if the weight of the world was holding him down. Until now, he couldn't understand why some people just gave up on life—on everything. But he was closer to understanding it now.

After making a cup of strong tea, he tried frying an egg in the small pan he found in the cabinet, worn from what looked like years of use and abuse. What started out to be an over-medium egg turned out scrambled. But it was good enough. He wanted to get an early start, and he wasn't in the mood to talk to anyone—not Lena, not anyone.

Taking his usual precaution, he wrote a note about his whereabouts and left it on his bed, just in case. He planned to hike today, but with a mission to explore the area around the old campground. After filling his backpack with the essentials for a day hike, he slipped outside to his truck, hoping no one would see him.

He took one of the roads he knew would get him close but at enough distance that he wouldn't be seen. He slung his backpack over his shoulders and adjusted the straps and clip buckles until the weight was comfortably centered on his back. His knife sheath was on his belt and a canister of bear spray in one of the outside pockets of his pack in case he needed it quickly.

After parking his truck, the walk to the campground area took about thirty minutes, as the terrain was uneven and Cody wanted to walk slowly enough to surveil the area, while making as little noise as possible.

Like the field from which Ayita disappeared, the campground area was mostly open and surrounded by trees and other growth around the perimeter. Cody would have to avoid walking out into the open and setting himself up for an ambush. Instead, he found a spot where he could settle in comfortably and watch from enough distance to feel safe.

Under different circumstances, Cody would have loved hiking in an area like this. The birds were singing, the sun was shining, and the gentle wind softly strummed the trees like an instrument.

After an hour passed with no activity, Cody reminded himself not to let his guard down. Besides, something was bugging him and he couldn't figure out what. While he didn't have all the pieces, those he did have just weren't adding up. And the worst part was that now he didn't know who to trust. Typically, he was able to rely on his instincts, but these people were strangers and he was an outsider, an unwanted one. The sideways glances and other unspoken signals they gave each other reinforced his standing in the community.

A small bug nibbled the back of his hand, and he thumped it into a nearby bush. As he turned his head, something caught his eye. Or more precisely, someone caught his eye. Although Cody wasn't close enough to study his face, he'd recognize that shape anywhere. Abe.

Cody crouched lower into the surrounding growth

and focused his binoculars on whatever was going on across the wide-open field. He saw movement but couldn't recognize any of the other faces, so he studied their shapes instead. He got a partial view of a man he didn't recognize and the shape of another person, who was mostly hidden by the small stand of trees they were using for cover.

Lowering his binoculars, Cody blinked several times before looking again. He wanted his vision as clear as possible because he was seeing something he didn't believe. The shape was one he had seen many times.

A sudden noise startled Cody, especially since it was coming from his side of the open area. There was no way to drive a car up that narrow path leading to this area. But an ATV could easily make the trip. And he soon realized that's exactly what he heard, an ATV.

Cody was far enough away from the path that no one would see him if he held perfectly still. He lowered his binoculars for fear the sun might reflect off the lenses and give him away. His heart was beating fast and his entire body was now on full alert. Slowly, he put his hand on the belt sheath and withdrew the hunting knife.

And then there was silence. The ATV had stopped not too far away and Cody now heard someone, or perhaps two people, stomping through the woods, getting closer.

Suddenly the noise of a whistle shattered the air, and several birds took flight. Across the way, on the other side of the field, two short whistles answered. The ATV then started up again and drove past Cody, not twenty feet from his hiding spot. It was close enough for Cody to see who was holding onto the steering wheel as it bounced over the rough terrain.

CHAPTER FORTY-SEVEN

Cody eased back further into the cluster of small trees and growth where he was hiding and raised his binoculars again. After crossing over the open area, Skip got out of the ATV and walked over to Abe.

The other figure Cody recognized was Maker. She seemed to be arguing with Abe. Without warning, he slapped her, nearly knocking her to the ground. He was too far away to hear their conversation, but it was obviously a heated exchange.

Without warning, a white panel truck drove up to join the small gathering from the other side of the field. It had entered from the only decent road to the campground, a dirt road that eventually wound its way back to a county road.

And then a sound Cody had not expected: a child's voice. It was female and didn't sound in distress. In fact, she was singing as she danced near the open field. Maker tried to run after her, but Abe put his arm out to stop her. Instead, Skip walked over to her and gently took the child's hand. Cody had never seen Ayita in person, but the girl matched the photo Lena had shown him.

Cody's head was throbbing, trying to sort through what he had seen. Was this group the "they" Kat had talked about? Were all of them involved in Ayita's abduction?

As Skip led Ayita back to the small gathering of people, two young women were being escorted into the truck by the man who had driven it. As far as Cody could tell, the women were not restrained in any way, but their shuffling feet and slumped shoulders suggested they had been drugged or perhaps beaten and threatened into submission.

Suddenly, that feeling of being overwhelmed washed over Cody again in a giant wave of despair. But he reminded himself he had no hard evidence that Ayita or anyone else was being held against their will.

After a few minutes, the truck started up again and the driver turned around in the open field and headed back down the dirt road. Cody refocused on Ayita. Skip took her by the arm and led her back to Abe. She wasn't struggling and wasn't in any distress that he could tell. Maker, however, was sobbing and appeared to be pleading with Abe about something, but he pushed her away. Maker then took Ayita by the hand and followed Skip back into the woods.

By the time Cody got back to the general store, it was approaching lunch time. Several people who looked like tourists were in the dining area. Cody reminded himself that he was just a visitor here himself, and if he wanted to, he could pack up his things and leave Raven's Rest, leave all this behind.

Even though Cody had spent years in law enforcement for the forestry service, he wasn't consumed with his work like some were. Sure, he wanted Ayita to be returned safely … but to whom? It seemed evident from what he had witnessed earlier that Maker was either in on the whole mess—or at the least, she was a silent witness.

On the positive side, Ayita looked as happy as everyone had described her to be before she disappeared. He wasn't sure saying she was "abducted" was accurate any longer.

He ordered a sandwich to go, deciding he needed to be alone to think through this new development.

Cody's phone rang just as he finished the last bite of lunch. The screen showed a New Mexico number.

"Mr. Hart, I'm sorry to bother you, but …" The woman sounded young and very nervous. "I'm with Aurora Path. I got your number from Nora's file. I hope you don't mind."

"What is it? Have you heard something about Nora?"

"She and I worked together. She was such a wonderful person." The woman cleared her throat. "But you know that already, I'm sure."

Growing impatient, Cody's voice was harsher than he intended. "You obviously have something to tell me. What is it?"

When the woman responded, her voice was so soft, like a whisper, that Cody could barely hear her. "I'm calling you because I know how much Nora loved you. And I know she would want—"

"What, dammit?" Cody snapped.

"The sheriff's office in North Carolina called here and then sent a photo asking our director if he could identify an Aurora Path t-shirt they found." She paused.

Cody felt sick to his stomach. "There must be hundreds of those shirts in circulation. Aurora Path helps runaways from all over the country, and they give those shirts out to them. So why did he call?" Cody asked.

"Because Nora's initials were marked on the label with a laundry marker. On really hot days, we often change shirts, so we make sure we have fresh ones available here. We have a small laundry area in the back and take turns washing the dirty ones. The initials help us sort them."

Cody's world was spinning out of control. "Where exactly did they find this t-shirt?"

"I know you're upset, and you should be, but I'm just trying to help. I don't know exactly where they found the shirt. I didn't talk to them, our director did, and she was told not to tell anyone until they have more information. The call was on speaker and I overheard it. I can't imagine what you're going through, Mr. Hart, but I thought you'd like to know. Please keep my name out of it. I could get fired."

Cody thanked her, his mind reeling with this new information.

"There's one more thing," the woman said. "You know they found Baxter Greene's body here in New Mexico, and that Nora was working with her, getting her counseling and a safe place to stay. Baxter didn't want to go back to North Carolina."

Getting impatient, Cody said, "Yes. Do you have any more details?"

"I've told the police everything I know. But I wanted to tell you that if someone came here to threaten Baxter, Nora would have protected her any way she had to. She was tenacious when it came to protecting her girls." Her voice lowered slightly. "But you know that."

"Are you suggesting Nora was …" Cody couldn't bring himself to say the words. "That she disappeared because she was helping Baxter?"

"I'm just saying, I know how Nora would react if someone came here trying to take Baxter. That's all. I've said enough now. And Mr. Hart, I hope you get good news on Nora soon."

CHAPTER FORTY-EIGHT

All Cody wanted to do now was to get everyone who knew even a scrap of information about Nora, Baxter, and Ayita together in one big room so everyone could share whatever they knew—no matter how small it may seem. He was tired of begging for information and trying to connect all the elusive dots.

He walked down to the general store to talk to Lena. "Got a few minutes?" he asked her.

"Sure, my assistant is working today. She can handle it for a little while."

Cody looked around to see who might be watching them. The recent revelations had made him suspicious of everyone. "Let's go talk in my cabin, if you don't mind."

Once they had settled inside, Cody glanced around his humble abode. When he had first moved in, it felt cozy and protective. Now, he was acutely aware he was in borrowed space—someone else's domain.

"If you don't mind me saying so, you look exhausted," Lena said.

Cody leaned forward, his arms on his thighs, and looked at the floor for a moment. "I am," he said finally. "And I need a friend."

Lena clasped her hands in her lap. "What's wrong, Cody? How can I help you?" And then her expression changed. "Oh, no. Have you heard . . . ?"

"No, I don't have any news about Nora. Well, I do, but it only adds to the confusion." He told Lena about the call and the discovery of Lena's t-shirt.

"You mean, here? That's where they found it?" Lena asked.

"I don't know exactly where, just that the center got a call from a NC sheriff's office." Cody looked up at the ceiling as if answers might magically appear there. "There's more," he said as he told her about seeing Abe, Skip, and Maker at the old campground field, as well as Ayita.

"What? Are you sure?" Lena asked.

One of the things he had learned about Lena was that she believed most people were good and would do the right thing. Life had taught Cody otherwise. "Yes, I'm sure. Kat hinted that several people were involved. Skip and Abe, and perhaps others, want to develop it into a luxury fishing resort." He paused. "Greed makes people do crazy things."

Lena leaned back in her chair and closed her eyes, likely praying that Cody had lost his mind and that nothing he had just said was true. "I just can't … I can't … but why?"

"Look, I don't know anyone around here well enough to trust them. But I trust you. What about Deputy Freeman? Can I trust him? Or should I go over his head?"

Lena looked shocked, as though Cody had slapped her in the face. "Why would you not trust him? Has he said or done anything to make you doubt him?"

Cody was afraid she might start crying. "Look, Lena, all I know is that my wife is missing and there are reasons to believe she might have been taken from New Mexico and brought here. And I know that a small child has been taken, with no knowledge or understanding of the fact that it's because she owns something other people want."

Lena's eyes filled with tears. "They killed Tucker, didn't they?"

Cody nodded. "It appears so." He cleared his throat. "Have you heard from Maker?"

Lena shook her head. "I hope she's alright." Wiping her eyes with the back of her hand, she asked, "What will you do now?"

"First of all, I'm going to demand answers from Freeman. And then if I have to, I'll go to his commander. All of this is bigger than one deputy, and if he doesn't realize that, then I've got to make him understand."

Lena walked over to Cody's chair and leaned down in front of him, taking his hands in hers. "What can I do to help?"

"Keep your eyes and ears open," Cody said. "I know it's not in your nature to distrust people, but we've got to be alert and suspicious of everyone right now."

Lena squeezed Cody's hands and released them. "Thank you for trusting me." A buzzing sound in her jeans pocket diverted her attention. "I'll just see who this is." When she pulled out her phone and looked at the screen, she said with a shocked look on her face, "It's Maker."

"Answer it," Cody said to Lena. "But don't let on I'm here."

Lena nodded and forced a slight smile as she answered the call. "Maker, how are you? We've all been worried about you." She tapped on the speaker icon on her phone so Cody could hear.

"I'm fine," Maker said. Cody could hear the strain in her voice. "Didn't mean to scare anyone."

"I went by your place and it looked like someone had broken in."

"I'll check on it when I get back. Probably kids from one of those Airbnb cabins."

Cody was listening intently, not just at what Maker was saying, but how her voice changed when she was lying. He motioned for Lena to keep Maker talking.

"Well, that's a shame. Would you like for me to report it—"

"No." Maker's voice betrayed her fear. "I mean, I'll take care of it. Deputy Freeman has got too much on his plate already, what with Ayita's disappearance and all the rest."

"So is there anything I can do to help?" Lena asked.

"No, I just wanted you to know I'm okay in case anyone asks. I'll be home when I can."

"Well, just be careful," Lena said.

Cody heard a noise, like a scuffling, in the background. And then Maker was gone.

"I'm calling Freeman right now," Cody said.

CHAPTER FORTY-NINE

As agreed, Cody met Freeman outside of Raven's Rest, in a neighboring town at a small tavern. When Cody arrived, he could barely see Freeman at a small back booth in the dimly lit area.

"Hey, man. You sounded upset," Freeman said. "What's going on?"

A young man appeared and took Cody's drink order. "You hungry?" Freeman asked Cody.

"No, I'm good," Cody said.

Freeman ordered a burger and fries and another IPA draft. "I missed lunch today. Sorry I couldn't meet you earlier, but I'm stretched thin."

"Thanks for meeting with me," Cody said. "I know that not everyone gets the same attention."

"Are you buttering me up for something?" Freeman asked.

Cody hesitated before answering. He didn't want to push Freeman away by being too demanding. Yet, Cody needed answers—and action—given the discovery of the t-shirt.

"I assume you're aware a t-shirt was found somewhere around here with Nora's initials on the label." It wasn't a question, because he knew that kind of information would have surely been passed on to Freeman.

Freeman looked uneasy. "Yes."

"When were you going to tell me?" Cody asked.

"First, tell me where you got the information?" Freeman asked.

Cody shook his head. "From a CI," he said, indicating a confidential informant.

Freeman surveyed the room before responding. "Look, man. I'm not even supposed to be talking to you. You're the victim's family, and I could get fired. And besides, I don't know the details, only that it was found."

Ignoring the deputy's comments, Cody asked, "Where did they find the t-shirt? Who found it? What are you doing to find my wife?" Cody could feel himself losing control and took a deep breath.

"It's out of my hands. The SBI is now officially involved in Nora's case," Freeman said.

Cody leaned back in his seat. "If the state police has taken the case, then you're confirming it was likely an abduction."

The server appeared with their food and drinks, and Cody impatiently waited until he was gone to continue. "Well?"

"Right now, nothing makes sense, but they're treating it as a possible abduction."

"And what about Ayita's case? Is it still considered an abduction too?" Cody asked.

Freeman shook his head and wiped his mouth with a napkin. "No, I thought you knew. Maker called to report Ayita has been found, said she had just run off and got lost. And since Maker is her legal guardian, the case will be closed."

Cody slammed his palms on the table, startling a

nearby server carrying a tray. "Funny, you don't look that dumb."

Freeman leaned back against the booth and raised his palms toward Cody. "Whoa, man. Take it easy."

Look, I'm telling you she's still being held for ransom. And Maker is somehow involved." Cody filled Freeman in on what he had observed at the campground and about seeing Abe strike Maker.

"You're way ahead of me," Freeman said. "I wish I had the time to follow every lead like you've done. But the reality is, I don't."

"Raven's Rest and its residents aren't worthy of your time. Is that about it?"

Freeman looked as if he was deciding how to respond. "Look, I'm officially off the case now that SBI is involved. I'll contact the special agent assigned to your wife's case and tell him what you just told me about Ayita. If she's still being held for ransom, then it's definitely something the SBI would handle. I'm just a small-county deputy sheriff." Freeman leaned back against the back of the booth. "I'm on your side. And I'm sorry I couldn't do more. You should be glad SBI is involved. They've got more manpower and a bigger budget."

Cody stood to leave and held out his hand. "Nothing personal. Just have them contact me right away."

"If Nora's alive, they'll find her," Freeman said.

CHAPTER FIFTY

When Cody's phone rang, it was 7 am. He didn't recognize the number on his phone screen but knew the 919-area code covered the Raleigh, North Carolina, area. When he answered, a man responded.

"Sorry if I woke you, Mr. Hart. This is special agent Eddie Benton, with the North Carolina State Bureau of Investigation."

Cody sat up in bed. "No problem. Thanks for contacting me."

"Actually, I'm sitting in the dining area of the general store right now. Can you join me for breakfast?"

"Sure. I'll be there in a few minutes, soon as I throw on some clothes," Cody said. He found his jeans on the floor where he had left them last night after meeting with Freeman and pulled a fresh shirt from his closet.

When Cody walked into the dining area, Lena made eye contact immediately and nodded her head toward a man sitting alone, sipping coffee. Cody approached the table. "Agent Benton?" Cody asked.

"Call me Eddie, like my friends do." He stood and shook Cody's hand with a firm, strong grip.

Cody sat down across from Eddie "Are you handling Nora Hart's case?"

Eddie nodded. "I just recently got it, but yes. And I want to say how sorry I am you're going through all this.

The uncertainty must be really hard for you."

Cody nodded. "Yes, it is."

"Again, I'm sorry to call you so early, but I wanted to meet with you while I was in town today."

Cody nodded. "No problem. You can call me anytime."

"I understand you met with Deputy Freeman last night."

"I was stressed and more than a little demanding, as he probably mentioned. But, yeah, we met."

"He called me on the way back from meeting with you, but I had planned to contact you today anyway."

Cody felt himself tensing. "Do you have more information?"

Eddie poured another cup of coffee from the carafe Lena had left on the table. "Before we get into the details, I have something I need to ask you."

Cody braced himself for another round of questioning. The New Mexico police had cleared him, but this was a different jurisdiction and a new ballgames. "Go ahead."

"Your record is impressive, and as you know, you're not considered a suspect in any way."

Cody's breathing eased.

"After Deputy Freeman filled me in on the assistance you've provided, I talked to my commander last night and to the county sheriff early this morning." Eddie smiled slightly. "He wasn't as understanding as you are about early calls." I proposed to them a temporary assignment for you. That is, if you're interested. We have a small discretionary budget, but I can pay you a meager consulting fee. More importantly, this arrangement would give me a legitimate way to share information with you. Of course, I'll also need to clear it with your CO in New Mexico."

Cody nodded. "I'm not interested in the money. What do you want me to do?"

"The SBI would like for you to serve as a wilderness and field expert on this case. I'll be honest, I'm not the outdoorsy type and know nothing about this area of the state. From all indications, whatever is going on is off the beaten path, to say the least."

"I'm still learning about this area myself."

Eddie grinned. "From what I hear, you're a quick study and won't stop until you get answers." His smile faded. "Since you're personally involved in this case, you'll have to maintain a certain, let's say, emotional distance if this assignment is going to work. Got it?"

Cody nodded.

"We don't know for sure if your wife is, or has been, in this area. Nor do we know if her case is in any way connected to the child's disappearance."

Cody nodded. "I'm definitely in. Thanks for including me."

"Don't thank me yet, and don't make me regret this offer, which is somewhat selfish on my part. I just didn't want to look stupid tromping around out here, not knowing the people or the land." He paused. "Now tell me about this young girl who was missing but is supposedly now back home and why you think her case is related to your wife's disappearance."

CHAPTER FIFTY-ONE

By the time Cody had filled Eddie in on all the possible connections of the two cases, Ayita's trust, his conversations with Kat and others, the breakfast crowd had all left the dining area.

"That's impressive work," Eddie said. "We need to first focus on the child, Ayita. Deputy Freeman says you don't believe she's been released."

Cody nodded. "As I said, I've seen her, and she appears to be fine. She likely has no idea what's going on."

"Well, before we get ahead of ourselves, I need to call your CO in New Mexico. You're on leave, right? Or did you resign?"

"On leave, for obvious personal reasons," Cody said.

"Do they know you're here? I wouldn't want to be the one to tell them."

"They're aware, but I haven't been checking in. No reason to."

Eddie stood up. "I'll just take care of this bill and then we'll meet back at your cabin in about an hour. That work?"

"I've got a running tab, so don't worry about the bill."

Eddie tipped two fingers to his forehead in a quick, informal salute and a show of respect for a fellow lawman. "Great. Thanks."

Lena came over to Cody's table as soon as Eddie had

left. "Well?"

"Well, I'm now a consultant on special assignment with the North Carolina State Bureau of Investigation."

Lena put her hand on Cody's shoulder. "That sounds mighty impressive, Mr. Cody Hart. Don't get the big head, you hear." She smiled. "This meal's on me, you know, to celebrate your new status." She put her finger to her lip and whispered, "But don't worry. I won't tell anyone."

As she started to walk away, Cody said, "Can you give me the phone number Maker called you from, and the time she called?"

Lena looked hesitant. "I'm not sure … I mean …"

"Lena, I know you don't want to get involved, but she called you, and you may have to give a statement later, depending on how all this goes down. And they may need to track her calls if she denies being at the campground. We just don't know at this point where all this is going to lead. Maker may be a victim—or a willing participant."

Lena pulled her phone from the back of her jean's pocket and tapped on recent calls. "Here," she said, handing the phone to Cody. And then, slightly smiling, she added, "I knew you'd be trouble from the day you showed up here."

"You've got good instincts," Cody said. He took a picture of her screen with his phone. "Got it." As he started to get up from the table, Lena put her hand on his arm. "Please be careful."

"I will. By the way, I haven't seen Abe around here. What excuse is he giving for being out of town so much?"

"Sick family is what he told me. Told me not to worry, that he'd be back soon."

Cody sighed. "You know, this could be a great little town, except for the trafficking, kidnapping, lies, and secrets."

CHAPTER FIFTY-TWO

After convening at Cody's cabin, he and Eddie set out in Cody's pickup, as the black SUV with the SBI emblem on it would be a bit obvious. Cody was glad to see Eddie had changed into clothes more suitable for tromping in the woods.

As Cody approached the old campground field, he took the same route he had before and they hiked to the place where Cody had previously observed the suspicious activity. "What's over there on the other side of this field?" Eddie asked, pointing.

"Probably the same as what's over here, just more woods. But then, I haven't explored deep into the property. Not sure who owns what around here, and I don't want to find out at the wrong end of a shotgun." Cody glanced at the gun on Eddie's belt. "You've got a little more protection than I have," he said patting his hunting knife sheath. "Since I'm out of my jurisdiction and on leave to boot, I don't tote my gun."

"Probably a good idea. Although, you're messing with some dangerous folks here."

Cody held his finger to this mouth. "Shh... I hear something." Several ravens flew overhead and landed in front of them in the field.

"Those are seriously big birds," Eddie said. "Guess that's where the town's name came from."

"Yep," said Cody. He trained his binoculars on the opposite side of the field.

"If you're right and they're shipping women from here, and maybe even men and children, we need to find out where they're holding these victims."

"Are you suggesting we go to the other side?" Cody asked. "Might be dangerous if we're caught. And they likely have field cameras set up on those trees. I can't see them from here but we'd have to get closer to be sure."

"And then it would be too late," Eddie added.

"Exactly." Cody surveyed the area again. "Let's go around to the river side. It's real shallow right over there," he said pointing. "And we can go downstream a way, see if there's any kind of structures around."

Eddie smiled. "Just what I was thinking. Lead on."

Cody shook his head. "You city folks." He pointed to Eddie's hiking boots that still looked brand new. "Those things waterproof?"

Eddie made a face. "Of course."

Cody led the way to the left and then after checking again to be sure no one was around, he made his way to the creek and stepped into the water. "Try not to splash too much."

After they had stepped carefully through the water for about fifty feet, Cody held up his hand for Eddie to stop. Then he put his finger to his mouth and whispered, "Shh ..."

The two men froze, remaining motionless. A black bear appeared ahead, foraging for food. "Just be still," Cody said as he pulled the bear spray from his pack. "He'll move on once he knows we're not a threat."

When the bear slowly ambled back into the woods, Cody motioned for Eddie to follow him. Stepping carefully while looking for bear traps, trip wires, or other devices rigged on the trail, Cody walked further into the wooded area. He pointed to the ATV tracks in the moist soil and followed them.

Cody moved slowly, scanning the terrain, eyes tracing every detail. "Check the trees for cameras," he said. Noticing a faint depression in the ground, Cody whispered, "Over here." He knelt, brushing away leaves and pine needles that looked like they had been placed there rather than naturally scattered. "This looks like it was an old mine entrance—probably from mica or feldspar operations years ago."

Cody pushed deeper into the foliage, his tracking instincts alert. The terrain dropped slightly, almost imperceptibly. It was another door, flush to the ground. But this one had been reinforced with relatively new timbers.

"If you want me to open this door, you need to be ready to use that thing," Cody said pointing to Eddie's gun.

Eddie rested his palm on the grip of his 9mm, thumbing the release lever on his holster and then nodded to Cody, signaling he was ready.

Cody slowly pulled the round metal handle on the door. It was heavier than he thought it would be, but he was able to get some momentum and swing it open. After seeing nothing but darkness below and hearing no voices, Cody took out his flashlight and aimed the beam down into the opening where a sturdy metal ladder descended into its depths. "Clearly, someone has been maintaining and using this entrance," he said. "I'm going down."

Eddie nodded, his jaw clenched.

Cody stepped carefully onto the ladder, testing each rung and shining his flashlight beam below. Shadows danced around the stone walls, some areas glistening with moisture on the rocky surfaces. The air was damp but not stale or musty.

"Cody," he heard Eddie whisper from above. "Come on back up. It's too dangerous."

"Give me another few feet." Cody descended a few more rungs, and as his flashlight beam swept over the stone surface, a glint caught his eye. He moved down another few feet until he could make out an industrial-style, metal box electrical switch, its housing bolted into the rock wall. Thick conduit snaked away from it, protecting the wires and disappearing into the darkness.

Logic told him if it was pitch black below him and this switch wasn't on, then nobody was waiting below. But it was a gamble.

"Cody," he heard Eddie say again, this time a bit louder.

Holding his breath, Cody flipped the switch, illuminating a large open area beneath him.

CHAPTER FIFTY-THREE

Cody was about five feet from the bottom of the metal ladder as he surveyed the open space below. The smart thing to do would be to go back up and get SBI reinforcements to come down and check it out. But maintaining a mineshaft wasn't illegal.

Suddenly, he heard ravens above, apparently near the entrance. As his instincts kicked in, Cody took a few steps back up the ladder, flipped off the switch and began climbing back up to the surface as quickly as he could safely do so. Losing his footing and tumbling down into whatever lay below was not an option.

The sound of an ATV's engine was getting louder. "Cody," he heard Eddie call.

"Coming up now," Cody said. He scrambled to the top, hoisting himself up and onto the ground above. Eddie, hand on his holster, was looking around.

"Come on," Cody said. "Let's get back to the river." He took a tree branch lying nearby and brushed their footprints the best that he could. An experienced tracker would easily notice their intrusion, but he hoped Abe and Skip would not. They might live in the mountains, but Cody didn't get the impression they were skilled outdoorsmen.

Cody and Eddie quickly reached the river and hid behind a cluster of small bushes and trees. Eddie slapped at a bug on his arm, causing Cody to smile. "What?" Eddie asked.

"Just thinking that our lives might depend on you being able to resist the urge to slap your arm."

Eddie grimaced. "Right, sorry."

Cody shifted his position slightly so he could see the area they had just left. Within seconds, the ATV Cody had seen earlier came into view. Skip shut off the engine and went to the rear cargo area. He picked up a cardboard box that appeared to be somewhat heavy by the way he was handling it.

Skip then took a rope attached to a large canvas sling from the ATV, placing the sling under and around the box. After opening the door, the same one Cody had just exited, Skip lowered the box into the opening and dropped the rope, appearing to have successfully delivered the box to its intended location down the shaft.

A nearby raven exploded from the low branch with a harsh kraaawk kraaawk, a warning that echoed through the trees. Unfazed by the raven's outburst, Skip climbed back onto the ATV and drove away.

When Cody was sure Skip was gone, he stepped out of the growth that was hiding them and motioned for Eddie to follow.

"Who owns this land?" Eddie asked.

"It's supposedly in a trust for Ayita, but I'm not positive where the boundaries are."

"We can't ask a judge for a search warrant because she's been reported safe now. And there's nothing we saw here today that's illegal. You said you saw her guardian with her, so our hands are tied."

"I'm not ready to give up, and I'm guessing they'll

wait until early tomorrow morning to move any human cargo they're holding," Cody said. "You up for another rendezvous tomorrow?"

Eddie grinned. "Gee, Cody, I didn't know you cared."

"We'll meet at my cabin early tomorrow and then come back here. Bring any fancy surveillance equipment or cameras you've got. We might need to document something."

"I need to report all this, just in case," Eddie said.

"And what would you report? That we're keeping an eye on a suspicious situation?"

Eddie shrugged. "Okay, let's just hope nothing goes wrong."

When Cody got back to the cabin, he sat on the edge of his bed and sipped a cold beer, savoring every swallow and thinking about something that had been bugging him all day. Some things just weren't adding up. He decided to call Kat and give her an update.

Kat didn't seem to be surprised when she answered, as if Cody was just a friend checking in. "It's good to hear from you," she said. Her cheerful tone made Cody wonder if she already knew about Ayita.

"I just wanted to let you know I saw Ayita," Cody said. "She appeared to be safe."

"Yes, Maker told me Ayita has returned. That's wonderful. I want to thank—"

Cody interrupted. "She hasn't returned. Maker was with her, but they're both with Abe and Skip."

There was such a long silence on the line that Cody thought they might have been cut off. "Kat?"

"Sorry. Did you say Ayita is not at Maker's house? That's what I assumed."

"I went by there today, on my way from …" Cody didn't want to get into the details of what he and Eddie had found at Maker's place earlier today. "Anyway, the house was dark. No one was there."

When Kat replied, her tone was much less cheerful. "Where did you see Ayita and Maker?"

"At the old campground. Can you confirm again that this land is in Ayita's trust?"

"Yes, it is," Kat said.

"Do you by chance have a plat of the land in the trust? I'd like to see the boundaries."

"I'll take a photo and send it after this call." There was a brief silence before Kat added, "Why did Maker lie to me?"

"Did she actually tell you Ayita was at home with her?"

"Well, I can't remember exactly how she said it, but that was certainly the impression I got." Another brief pause, then, "She lied. Plain and simple. That makes me angry and very suspicious."

Cody debated with himself before replying. "I can't be sure, but it appeared that Maker was being held there. I saw Abe slap her to the ground."

"I'll send that photo right over," Kat said before she abruptly ended the call.

CHAPTER FIFTY-FOUR

At dawn the next morning, Cody and Eddie positioned themselves on the opposite side of the field, as they had before. But no activity had been seen, and Cody was beginning to think this stakeout wouldn't yield anything useful.

Another hour passed, and Cody had nearly dozed off in his hiding spot when a noise in the background became louder. "Eddie, you awake?" Cody whispered.

Eddie sat up straighter. "What's happening?"

Cody put his hand to his ear. "Hear that?" By now, the sound of an approaching vehicle was distinct. Within a minute, the same white panel truck Cody had seen earlier came into view. The driver got out and appeared to be calling someone on his cell phone as he glanced around the area.

Eddie got his camera with its telephoto lens into position and began snapping shots, adjusting the range periodically.

"Keep shooting," Cody said.

The sound of an ATV was now distinct—and was approaching. When it came into view, Skip was driving and had a young female sitting beside him. Eddie continued to take shots. "Turn your head," he whispered, as if trying to send a message to the girl. "Let me see your face." Suddenly, he broke into a grin. "Yes! Got it."

Cody reached for the camera and looked into the viewer. "She's what, maybe sixteen or so? Native American, or at least similar features of dark hair and eyes." He handed the camera back to Eddie. "Keep shooting."

Skip got out of the ATV and went around to the other side, grabbing the girl's arm and pulling her out of the vehicle. She didn't object and appeared to be sedated. Her hands were secured in front of her by a zip tie.

"What are you planning to do?" Cody asked. "We've got to rescue her."

"Whoa. I'm not charging in there without backup. And neither would you, if you were in command."

Cody didn't reply but recalled the number of times he had done exactly that. Foolish, yes, but when he felt it was his responsibility to act, he did.

"I'll call for a helicopter to surveil them from a distance so as not to be obvious," Eddie said. "Maybe we can find out where they're headed."

"Can you also get them to scan those woods? They don't appear to be keeping the girls in the mine we found. Probably just a storage site for supplies."

After the girl was put in the back of the panel truck, Skip went into the woods and returned with a cardboard box, similar to the one they had seen him lower into the mine yesterday. Skip and the truck driver then talked briefly and the truck pulled away, headed out the same way it came in. Eddie called in the information and asked for immediate helicopter support but was told there wasn't one available due to other operations in progress.

"Damn!" Cody said. "They're going to get away. We need to follow them."

Eddie put his hand on Cody's arm. "First of all, unless you know otherwise, the road we came in on and that road over there are *not* the same road. And they don't appear to intersect in any way. How do you plan to get over there without driving across this field?"

While Cody didn't reply, his frustration was obvious.

Without explanation, Eddie called a number again. "How about drone support?" he asked. "We've got a critical situation here and a girl's life may be at stake." He gave them the information and GPS coordinates. When the call ended, Eddie said, "They're doing a scan of an area suspected to be a meth lab. It's not far away, so they'll be here soon."

"So what do we do now?" Cody asked.

"We wait."

CHAPTER FIFTY-FIVE

"Waiting is the worst part of the job," Eddie said, peering through the telephoto lens. "All's quiet over there now." He lowered the camera. "It's not a big operation. If it was, we'd see dozens of victims. You said you saw only one earlier, and this morning there was only one."

"That we saw, at least," Cody said. "That's why they haven't been caught. Small operation, easier to stay under the radar. They make a little cash here and there until they can build their trout fishing resort all over this area," he said with a sweeping motion of his arm. "All this will be developed one day. If not by Abe and Skip, then by someone else."

"But you said the land is in Ayita's trust," Eddie said.

"It is." Cody reached in his pocket. "I almost forgot, Kat sent me this photo of the land plat. All of this is owned by Ayita—unless Kat gives in to the ransom and hands it over."

Eddie's jaw tightened. "That's not going to happen. Not on my watch."

"Kat's pretty upset with Maker for misleading her and implying Ayita was home." Cody put his hand on Eddie's arm. "Shh. I hear something." In the distance, there was a slight hum, like an angry mosquito on the hunt for fresh blood.

Before Eddie could respond, he got a call from SBI saying they had a drone in the area. "No, we didn't get a plate for the panel truck," he said to the caller. "And it's white, like a million others. Hey, you got more than one unit here?" Eddie listened and nodded affirmatively for Cody's benefit. "Have the second unit check out the wooded area across the field." He told the caller about the mine shaft. "There's likely a holding place somewhere nearby, but those woods are dense. And it's too risky to go charging in there, not knowing what kind of detection and artillery they've got." Eddie listened for a moment and then ended the call. "They'll let us know if they observe anything of interest," he said to Cody.

"Well, I guess we wait now." Then Cody added, "I'm not very good at waiting though."

Eddie leaned back against a nearby tree trunk. "While we're waiting, tell me more about your wife. Deputy Freeman told me a little, and I'm sorry. Must be awful, not knowing."

Cody stared off into space momentarily with what some call the thousand-yard stare. "Yeah, it's rough. And I keep imagining different scenarios that drive me crazy."

"Did you think you'd find her here in Raven's Rest?" Eddie asked. "That's a long way from New Mexico."

"Exactly. That's the point. Nobody would be looking for her here, not like they were back home where her picture was posted everywhere, and where they exhausted every lead." He looked away briefly. "If they did bring her here ..." He swept his arm around. "Look around this place. If they disposed of a body here, no one would find it, at least not for a very long time. Hunters don't come to this area, and the nearby towns are sparsely populated. I'd venture to say most people from Raven's Rest rarely come up here, if ever. At least not since the campground closed. Why would they?"

"But then why not dispose of her somewhere along the way? There's a lot of miles between here and New Mexico."

Cody took a moment to respond. "That's what drives me crazy. If they killed her along the way, where is her body? And if they didn't, then what did they do with her?"

Eddie cleared his throat. "Sounds like you had a great marriage," he said, in an obvious effort to change the mood. "I had two wives, but neither of them put up with me for very long."

"Nora is amazing," Cody said. "We used to know what the other person was thinking and finish each other's sentences. It scared me sometimes how close we were … because of something like this. I knew I couldn't handle it if something happened to her."

Eddie gently tapped Cody's arm with his fist. "When we get these bastards, we'll find out where she is. Okay?"

Cody nodded. "I got time and nothing else to lose."

CHAPTER FIFTY-SIX

Eddie's phone vibrated again, and he answered, barely louder than a whisper. "Roger that, thanks," he relied.

"They find the truck?" Cody asked.

Eddie shook his head. "They got too much of a head start. We'll try again tomorrow. The helicopter is going to surveil the area again, but there's no use for us to stay here. We can't go charging across the field like the cavalry." Eddie punched Cody's arm playfully. "Right, buddy?"

Without responding, Cody stood up and brushed dried leaves off his jeans. Eddie stood up and followed him to the pickup.

After riding silently for a short distance, Cody asked, "Where are you staying tonight? You know, in case we get some information and need to get back out here?"

"We are not, I repeat, you and I are not going out there alone. I know you think this is a small-time operation, and it does appear to be. But their bullets work just as well as any other thug's." Cody remained focused on the road without replying. "Once we have a location, if there is one, we'll have backup to go in, people who are trained to do so. Got it?"

Again, Cody remained silent.

"Look, man, I can't even imagine the emotions you must be feeling right now. I'd be crazy if my wife …" Eddie paused and looked out the window briefly. "There's a reason lawmen are removed from cases involving family members. I got permission to get you involved so you could help us find Ayita. Anything else is a bonus. Got it?"

Cody nodded.

"Don't make me regret bringing you in on this operation. Okay?"

Cody again nodded. After a moment, he said, "You're welcome to bed down in my cabin. I saw an air mattress in the storage space outside. I'm used to bedding down on the ground."

Eddie smiled. "You just want a drinking buddy tonight. Am I right?"

Cody looked at Eddie and smiled slightly. "You'd better not snore."

Cody and Eddie, having decided to have dinner at the store's diner when they returned, sat at a table near the back. Eddie insisted on having a clear view of the door. "Old habits," he said to Cody.

Cody nodded. "I do the same."

After they ordered dinner from their server, Cody saw Lena and walked over to talk to her. In a moment, she followed him back to the table. Cody nodded toward Eddie. "Just wanted to let you know, he's staying at the cabin tonight. Hope that's okay with you."

Lena nodded. "Of course. Any luck today?"

Before Cody could respond, Lena nodded her head toward the entrance. Abe walked in and sat by himself at one of the front tables. "That son of a …" Cody muttered softly.

Lena and Eddie exchanged glances, as though they were deciding which of them should intervene. Lena put her hand on Cody's shoulder. "I need to get back to work."

"It's like he knows we're on to him and doesn't care," Cody said.

"Let's just enjoy a nice meal and go chase the bad guys tomorrow, cowboy. I'm tired and it could be another long day of waiting." Eddie stood up. "Excuse me. I'll be right back."

Cody nodded, assuming Eddie was going to the restroom, but then he saw him motioning for Lena to follow him into the kitchen. Cody glanced at Abe to see if he was watching them, but he was staring down at his phone screen and appeared to be texting.

The food had arrived and Cody was eating when Eddie came back to the table and sat down. "Your food's getting cold," Cody said. "Anything you want to fill me in on?"

"Just trying to make our work a little easier," Eddie said.

Cody looked up and studied Eddie's face for a clue. "Oh? And how's that?"

Eddie took a large bite of burger and said with his mouth half-full, "Lena pointed out Abe's truck." He chewed a few times. "Got a tracker on him now."

CHAPTER FIFTY-SEVEN

The next morning, Eddie sat up in the small bed and stretched. "Well, did I snore?"

"All night," Cody said. "Want breakfast? Or I've got a couple protein bars we can have. I'll make some coffee."

Eddie stood and pulled on his trousers. "Much as I'd like to experience Lena's cooking again, we need to get out there early." He held out his hand. "So yeah, give me one."

Cody handed him a protein bar and Eddie unwrapped it and took a bite. "Not too bad for healthy food." He took another bite. "But it's definitely not bacon and eggs."

Less than thirty minutes later, Eddie and Cody were driving up the steep mountain road to the backside of the old campground. As Cody parked his truck a short distance away behind a stand of trees, he said, "There's a reason they use the other side, you know." He waved his arm around. "Look around here. There's nowhere to hide."

"We'll get them soon enough. We just need more than a few suspicious looking photos of a young woman, who could, by the way, be a relative. Or a sick friend."

"With their hands zip tied?" Cody turned to look at Eddie. "Does everyone at SBI have stupid thoughts like that? Or is it just you?"

Eddie smiled. "They're all smarter than me. Now be quiet and let's get into position." He glanced at his wristwatch, a military style with a black face that had numerous dials on it. Eddie raised his wrist nearer to his face and spoke softly. "We're in place."

Pointing above, Eddie said to Cody, "The helicopter is about to make a pass."

Cody looked up and nodded but didn't see anything yet.

Eddie held his wrist up to his ear again and listened. Cody couldn't make out what the person was saying, and Eddie was just nodding. "Copy that," Eddie said. He turned to Cody. "You're right. There's an old building, looks like an abandoned barn, deep in those woods. There's a narrow dirt road nearby that leads back to the state road." He paused. "And our eyes in the sky says he saw a few women being loaded into a white panel truck. They couldn't make more than one pass or it would give them away. They flew as high as they could to avoid an appearance of surveillance. But that also means less visibility."

"So what happens now?" Cody asked.

"We'll show the photos to the brass and get permission to investigate further and maybe raid the building. But I'm not too hopeful. You know how slow the wheels of justice turn." He paused. "And remember, we don't officially have a victim."

Cody closed his eyes and took a few deep breaths. He was very familiar with the constraints of law enforcement, but he still didn't like it.

The sound of an approaching vehicle broke the silence. "That building must not be too far away. Unless that's a second truck," Eddie said, peering through his binoculars. "Wait. It's a Range Rover. Anybody you know drive one?"

Cody reached out and took the binoculars from Eddie. He blinked a few times to sharpen his focus and looked again. "That's Kat, Ayita's aunt. What's she doing here?"

Suddenly the panel truck drove up, pulled around the Range Rover and parked. Abe jumped out of the truck and began yelling at Kat. They were too far away to hear all their words, but Abe was clearly upset and waving his arms in the air. Was Kat part of this scheme also? But she's the one who set up the trust for Ayita. Maybe Kat changed her mind and decided to sell the land and make a big profit. All these questions were swirling in Cody's mind when he heard a woman scream.

Cody started to stand but Eddie put his arm out to stop him. "Wait," Eddie said. "Don't blow this operation until we know what's going on."

CHAPTER FIFTY-EIGHT

Cody watched the confrontation between Abe and Kat through his binoculars. "We've got to go in before they hurt Kat."

Eddie put his hand on Cody's arm. "Wait. We need to know if she's involved or what her role is here."

Cody reluctantly agreed, as he watched what appeared to be a heated argument between Kat and Abe. Suddenly, Abe grabbed her by the arm and slung her to the ground like a rag doll. For an old man, he appeared to be fairly strong. He then got in the truck and drove away, leaving Kat on the ground.

When Abe was down the road and out of sight, Kat managed to get up. She walked slowly back to the Range Rover, limping slightly.

Without warning, Cody took off sprinting across the field. Kat was backing up and preparing to go back down the road when Cody pounded his fist on her rear window. She stopped the vehicle, and Cody ran around and jumped into the passenger seat. "Keep going," Cody said as he slumped down in the seat.

"What the hell are you doing here?" Kat asked.

"That's what I was going to ask you," Cody said.

"I thought I might be able to talk some sense into that mean son of a bitch. He says they're shipping Ayita out today, to a buyer, because I won't sign the trust over to them."

"Why not just give the land to them and then fight it once you have Ayita back?" Cody asked.

"Because I don't think they plan to live up to their end of the bargain. They'll never release her. Once the land is transferred, I'm afraid ..."

Cody looked around to see if anyone was following them. "How did you know they'd be here? At this location?"

"I knew they wouldn't be closer into town. And I know Abe owns the land adjacent to this place." She lowered her voice slightly. "Not long ago, before Ayita was taken, Maker told me she suspected they were transporting human cargo from the old campground."

"Do you know where an old barn is near here?" he asked. "Probably on Abe's or Skip's property."

Kat nodded. "I think that's where they're holding Ayita. It looks abandoned from the outside, but Abe told Maker there are several small rooms, toilet facilities, and a kitchenette area. He claimed he rents the barn out to tourists looking for an 'authentic' mountain experience." She shook her head. "I doubt that."

"You've been inside?"

"No."

Cody pointed to the road ahead. "Where does this road go?"

"Nowhere now, or at least not far. There was a landslide years ago, and a portion of the road is closed. Because it wasn't used often, the state just abandoned it. At least that's what the newspapers reported."

"Then how do Abe and Skip get around? I saw them

leave the campground, just like you're doing."

"I'm going to show you." Kat drove a short distance until the road ended and then pointed to a dirt road, its entrance partially hidden by trees with low-hanging branches. Several ravens were perched on the ground across the entrance, appearing to be standing guard.

Cody looked at Kat again. "And you just happen to know about this road?"

She stopped the vehicle suddenly and turned to Cody. "Are you seriously suggesting I'm in on this?"

"Look I'm just trying to figure out who the bad guys are, and you seem to know a lot about this area."

"I've been here several times with Sterling, my attorney, to inspect the land and boundaries for the trust. These days, you also have to watch for squatters who take over vacant land and houses."

"Do you think Maker is part of their scheme?" Cody asked.

Kat leaned back against the headrest and sighed. "I don't believe Maker was part of the kidnapping plan. But she likely figured it out, confronted Abe, and tried to convince him to return Ayita. She and Abe have a strange, complex relationship that I've never understand." She paused. "But the fact that she lied to me is disturbing."

"I saw him knock her to the ground, so yeah, that's a strange relationship. He seems to like hitting women." Cody said.

"It's in his nature to abuse women." Kat pointed to the dirt road ahead. "This road veers off to the right after a short distance. That's Abe's property down there and where the barn is. The left side of the fork will take you back to the state road, where you come out on the other side of the closed section."

"Does Abe own this spot, where we are right now?"

Kat shook her head. "No. Ayita does."

CHAPTER FIFTY-NINE

Cody got out of the Range Rover and walked a short distance before returning to Kat. "How far down the road is it to the barn?" he asked.

"I'm not good at estimating distances, but it should be an easy walk."

Cody pulled out his cell phone, which he had silenced earlier, and noticed multiple texts from Eddie. Cody replied to the latest one and explained he was with Kat and that she would text him their location.

As Cody expected, Eddie immediately demanded that he return, to which Cody replied, "Send backup. Ayita being moved today."

Cody then gave Eddie's number to Kat and instructed her to explain the road situation to him. "I'll drive you there," she said. "You can't go in alone."

"I'm not putting you in any more danger than you're already in. I'll be fine. Just tell Eddie where we are. Give him the GPS coordinates from your phone."

"You have a gun, right?"

Cody patted the large hunting knife on his belt. "Do you by any chance happen to have one in the car?"

Kat reached behind the seat for a large tote-style leather purse. "I have this for protection." She handed him a small, .380 pistol with lavender grips.

"Jesus, Kat. Has anyone told you this little thing won't

stop anyone? All you're gonna do is piss them off." He looked at the gun again. "And lavender?"

Kat shrugged. "I wasn't planning on getting into a gun battle." Her chin protruded slightly. "And I happen to like lavender." She held out the pistol. "Take it anyway. There's a full clip in it and it might come in handy."

Cody took the gun. "After you text Eddie, get out of here and go someplace safe. Maybe Lena's store. But stay in touch with Eddie." He looked down the road and took a deep breath. "I'll do everything I can to get Ayita home."

"Thank you."

Cody got out, tucked the pistol in his back jeans pocket and began walking. He hoped Kat's "easy walk" meant less than a mile. Time was of the essence and if he tried to run the mile, he'd be too exhausted to do what he needed to.

As Cody walked along the side of the road, always on the lookout for a place to hide if needed, he thought about all that had brought him to this point in time, to this place. And then he pushed it out of his mind. He needed all senses focused on this mission.

Cody glanced at a raven that seemed to be following beside him. "Hey, buddy. You coming along as backup?" The raven answered with the now familiar kraaawk kraaawk as it kept following.

After what seemed like an eternity, Cody saw the fork ahead that Kat had mentioned. He was thankful to see that the right side had far more trees and natural coverage than the left side, the side that led back to the open portion of the state road. He checked carefully and trotted across the road to a large tree and hid behind it. The raven sounded off again, causing Cody to jump slightly. As he looked closer, the raven began walking down an overgrown path near the road but far enough from it to be a safer, less conspicuous route. It turned back to look at Cody as if asking, "You coming?"

Cody smiled and whispered, "Okay, buddy. I'm going to follow you, but you'd better not be in cahoots with them. Remember Ayita, the little girl who fed you in the field and danced for you? Well, she's in trouble and I've got to try to rescue her. So if this is a better way to the barn, let's go." *What is wrong with me? I'm talking to a raven and asking it for help.*

Cody dutifully followed the raven down the path. At one point, the path was so overgrown the raven flew up onto a tree branch. Thinking maybe this was where the path ended, Cody looked around for another route, but the raven flew ahead and swooped down.

Cody carefully stepped through the thick growth that covered the path until he could see where it resumed ahead, right where the raven was sitting, waiting for Cody to catch up. *When I find Nora, I'll have to tell her about these ravens. She loves animals so much.* Cody pushed those thoughts aside.

CHAPTER SIXTY

Within a few minutes, the old barn Kat had described was in front of him. It was rundown enough on the exterior that no one would suspect anything going on inside. That is, other than the satellite dish on the roof alongside solar panels. This place wasn't totally off the grid.

Crouching down in the undergrowth, Cody saw no signs of activity. After looking for security cameras, he carefully made his way to the back of the barn. A white panel truck sat under a crude canopy made of military-style camo netting stretched over upright wooden posts, making the vehicle undetectable from the air.

As Cody made his way completely around the barn, he found no signs of anyone. On the side hidden from the road, he found a sliding window that was unlocked. Carefully, he eased it open. Inside was a large room with two sofas, a few chairs, and other odd pieces of furniture. A floor lamp illuminated a portion of the room. The window Cody had opened was over the sink in a small kitchen area. He deep a deep breath and hoist himself through the large window. Thankfully, there were no dishes in the small sink, so Cody put his foot in it as he climbed through the window. With one foot firmly planted in the sink, he eased his other leg through the window and onto the laminate counter. He managed to get himself fully inside and then onto the kitchen floor.

With his back to the wall and Kat's lavender pistol in his hand, he carefully made his way to a small hallway where an extension to the barn had been added. He took a few steps toward a closed door, thinking momentarily about an old quiz show where the announcer asked, "What's behind door number one?" Cody could hold his own in a fight, but not against heavily armed men. But it was now or never.

Saying a silent prayer, Cody tried the door handle. It was locked. He tried again, wishing he had his lock pick set with him. But it was in New Mexico.

A faint noise behind the door caught his attention. Footsteps? Was this a bedroom—or something else? Then he heard a faint singing voice, a child's soft, sing-song voice.

Without giving himself time to think about the consequences if he guessed wrong, he tapped on the door. "Ayita?" he asked softly.

Only silence from behind the door now. Again, Cody tapped lightly on the door. "Lena sent me to bring you home."

Again, there was only silence. He was about to walk away when he heard a small voice. "I can't open the door. It's locked."

Cody again took several deep breaths to steady his nerves. "I'm going to get something to force it open. Okay?"

"Abe will be mad."

"It's okay. I'm going to get you out. Are you ready to go home?"

"Yes, sir." And then she added, "I wasn't bad. I stayed

here until Maker got better. That's what Abe said, that she was too sick to take care of me."

Cody's heart was pounding. If something went wrong, neither of them would ever go home again. He went to the kitchen to look for a knife or anything that could be used to get into that room. He couldn't find anything useful so he went back to the door. "Do you know where Abe is and the people who are keeping you here?" he asked.

"They leave me here by myself most days. Sometimes I get scared."

Cody reminded himself not to get emotional. *Stay focused.* "I'm going outside to see if I can find something to jimmy this lock. I'll be right back."

Rather than risk falling or slowing himself down by going back out the window over the sink, Cody opted to leave by the front door. He opened it carefully. As he was about to peer outside, something on the wall caught his eye: a lone key on a length of worn shoelace, hanging on a nail.

Cody snatched the key in his hand, praying it was *the* key. He walked quickly back down the hall. "I'm back. I'm going to try this key I found. Just stand back a little, away from the door, in case I have to shove it. Okay?"

"I will," the small voice said.

Cody wiggled the key into the door lock and tried to turn it. The door didn't open. Holding his breath, he tried again, this time forcing the key as far to the left as he could. He breathed a sigh of relief when he heard the tumbler click.

He slowly pushed the door open. A small girl stood a few feet away. It was clearly the same girl he had seen in

Lena's photographs. He leaned down to meet her eyes. "Ayita, I'm Cody."

Her sudden rush toward him caught him off-guard. When she threw her arms around him, her skin was soft and warm, and he could feel the wetness of her tears on his neck. "Let's go home, baby girl."

CHAPTER SIXTY-ONE

Cody gently pried Ayita's arms from around his neck. "We've got to get out of here, and I need for you to be brave. And very quiet. Okay?"

Ayita nodded.

"You stay close behind me and if I tell you to do something, you do it as quickly as possible. Understand?"

Again, she nodded.

Cody put his hand on her shoulder. "You're a brave girl." He motioned for her to follow him. "Don't talk," he whispered as he walked back to the path he had taken coming to the barn.

But before they made it back to the overgrown path Cody had followed, he heard a vehicle motor and then a man's voice: Abe's. "Hey, you. What the … "

Cody grabbed Ayita's hand and whispered, "Run into the woods," he pointed. "Over there. And wait. I'll come get you." Abe was approaching quickly. "But if I don't, just follow the path until you get to the road. Okay?"

Without responding or looking back, Ayita took off running. Cody pulled the pistol from his pocket just as he heard a bullet hit a nearby tree.

"Son of a bitch," Abe yelled. "I'm gonna kill your sorry ass."

Thankfully, Abe had some age on him, was overweight, and moved slowly. Cody crouched beside a large tree and released the safety on Kat's pistol. He waited until the man got closer, as the small pistol would have limited range and accuracy.

And then another vehicle approached. A gray Jeep Wrangler with Skip behind the wheel. He jumped out and pulled a pistol from his holster. "What's going on?" he yelled.

As Abe approached Cody and got uncomfortably close, Cody took careful aim and fired at his chest. But being unfamiliar with the gun, he missed. Abe fired back.

The shot landed high in Cody's left shoulder, and the impact knocked him sideways. Cody had been shot twice before in the line of duty while apprehending poachers and suspected murderers in the forest, so he knew the feeling of being shot: a hot steel rod, sharp, and then a deep, spreading throb. He tested his fingers and still had movement. Good sign. But his arm was getting numb and would soon be useless.

As warm blood soaked his shirt, Cody pressed his right hand over the wound, trying to slow the flow. Shock hadn't fully set in, but he could feel its edge: tunnel vision, heart hammering. He forced a breath in through his nose, slow and measured. *Stay alert. Assess. Act.*

In that moment, time seemed to stand still. Was this it? Was he going to die out here in these mountains in the middle of nowhere? Would Ayita simply be recaptured and … *And what about Nora?*

Cody could barely see Abe now. Was he readying himself to fire another shot? The kill shot?

"Stop. Lay down your weapon." The voice came from somewhere close by. Cody then heard more shots. And several more. And then a dark shroud covered him and the earth reached up and pulled him down, into its damp, cool embrace.

CHAPTER SIXTY-TWO

The voice sounded like it was a million miles away. "Co-dy." Darkness still shrouded his world. Was he dead? "Cody," the disembodied voice said again.

Slowly and with much effort, Cody opened his eyes as his world came back into focus. "Eddie?"

"You're fine, buddy. A helicopter's in the campground and will take you to the hospital. You'll be fine," Eddie repeated.

One by one, the details came back to him. "What ...?"

"You've been shot, but the bullet doesn't appear to have hit anything that won't heal." Eddie smiled, pointing to Kat's gun lying nearby. "That your cute little lavender gun over there?" But Cody didn't understand what Eddie was talking about. The dark shroud was hovering, threatening, waiting to cover Cody's world again. He felt a slight slap on his cheek.

"Cody, stay awake. You've lost a lot of blood, but hang in there," Eddie said. And then in a louder voice, he yelled to someone Cody couldn't see. "Over here. Here."

Cody tried to talk. "Ayi ..."

"The girl is fine. We found her crouching in the woods. Funny thing, she was singing, all quietlike, to a raven when we found her. She kept saying she was waiting for Maker to come back to get her and take her home. She thinks Abe was her babysitter."

Cody felt himself being hoisted onto a stretcher as he fought to stay awake. "Nora?"

Eddie patted Cody's leg and shook his head. "You just focus on getting well."

Eddie watched as the helicopter ascended from the open field and prayed Cody would make it. Why had Cody taken off with Kat and then gone in alone? It was almost as if he had a death wish.

Abe's lifeless body lay nearby. But Skip had managed to slip away, likely down one of the dirt roads and paths that only the locals knew. A second helicopter was circling above trying to find Skip or the white panel truck, but the dense forests made overhead surveillance difficult.

Ayita was being taken to Mission Hospital in Asheville to be checked for signs of injury or abuse. Maker was nowhere to be found, so Eddie called Lena who agreed to meet with the doctors at the hospital as Ayita's surrogate guardian.

Eddie signaled for one of the SBI agents. "We need to check that mine shaft, make sure no one is down there. And make sure we comb that barn for prints, anything."

"We've got the barn covered. Two agents are in there processing it now."

Eddie nodded and began walking, motioning for the man to follow. Within minutes they were standing at the concealed mine shaft he and Cody had explored. Eddie brushed away the leaves and pulled the wooden hatch open. "There's a ladder leading down into this shaft," Eddie said to the other SBI agent. "And a light switch mounted onto the rock wall a little further down."

"Wanna flip for who goes down?" the agent said smiling.

"I already did, and you lost," Eddie said. "Just be careful. And get that light on as soon as you find it."

Eddie watched as the man disappeared into total darkness. He could hear the agent's boots clanking on the metal ladder. Within moments, a faint light partially illuminated the shaft. "You okay down there?" Eddie called out.

When the agent didn't answer, Eddie called out again. "Hey, let me know what you see down there."

"Hold on," the agent said. "I'm … Holy crap." His voice sounded far away.

"You need me to come down?" Eddie asked.

"No, we need to get crime scene down here. There's a body. Female."

Eddie's chest tightened. "Old? Young?" he called down to the agent. "Are you sure she's dead?"

"I'm coming up," the agent called out. "The smell is awful down here."

CHAPTER SIXTY-THREE

Nearly an hour had passed since the forensics team had gone down the mine shaft to retrieve the body. While a positive identification had not been made, Eddie felt sure it was Maker, given the apparent age and stature of what was clearly a female. She had not been dead long.

The periodic updates from the helicopter overhead searching for Skip frustrated Eddie. How could someone disappear, just vanish, like Skip had? His thoughts then drifted back to Cody, who had likely asked that same question about Nora—probably hundreds of times. While Eddie didn't feel good about their chances of finding Nora, he tried to remain optimistic for Cody's sake. But Cody was a lawman and knew the odds.

Eddie got another message from the county deputy who was staking out Skip's real estate company in Asheville. According to the report, Skip was MIA and the office manager claimed she had no idea where he might be.

"Hey," an agent called out to Eddie. "We found this in the mine too."

Eddie took the small plastic evidence bag from the agent and examined it. It appeared to be a silver bracelet with a single charm, a heart, dangling from it. Working through the plastic evidence bag, he turned the charm over and saw the initials "NH" engraved on the back.

He handed the bag back to the agent. "Do me a favor.

Don't mention this to Cody just yet. I don't want to get his hopes up."

"I don't know him, but from what I've heard he's one of the good guys," the deputy said. "He must be going crazy looking for his wife, her just vanishing like that." He shook his head slowly. "Can't imagine what I'd do in his shoes."

Eddie took a photo of the bracelet. "I'll tell him and see if he can identify it. Just log it as evidence for now."

Another agent approached Eddie. "We're still searching the mine, but it appears to be a storage area, lots of metal shelving, canned goods, ammunition, survivalist kind of supplies. Also a couple of Army style bunk beds."

"It may be a holding area for human transport," Eddie said. He then walked back down the dirt road to the barn where Ayita had been held. Somewhere around a half dozen agents and forensics personnel were taking prints, bagging evidence, and searching every nook and corner. "Find anything?" he asked the lead agent.

"Not sure, but we're bagging everything."

"Find evidence of anyone else, other than the child, being held here?" Eddie asked.

The agent motioned for Eddie to follow him to the bathroom. "Found these in here." He pointed to a box of tampons.

Eddie rubbed his neck with his hands. "Geez. This just keeps getting better." He turned to leave. "I'll leave the search to you, but I want a report on what you've found asap."

"Roger that," the agent replied.

As Eddie was making his way back to the field area,

his phone vibrated. When he looked at the screen, he was surprised to see Cody's name. "Hey, buddy, you still alive?" Eddie asked.

"It'll take more than a bullet to stop me. Where're you now?"

"Whoa, buddy. If you've got any crazy ideas of coming back out here, forget it. Your assignment right now is to heal. Everything else is being taken care of," Eddie said. "Are you being admitted to Mission?"

After a brief silence, Cody answered, "Nah. I'm going find Ayita, get a ride back, and then crash at the cabin."

Eddie sighed. "Alright, if you insist on leaving, just wait there and I'll come get you."

"Sure," Cody said. "Thanks for everything. I mean it."

CHAPTER SIXTY-FOUR

To the protests of his nurse, Cody convinced her to help him put his shirt back on. "Mr. Hart, this shirt is bloody. You can't walk around the hospital in it. It's not, well, sanitary."

Cody glanced down at the front of his shirt. "Well then, I'll just keep this lovely hospital gown on. With my jeans, of course," he said, trying to smile at her. He was in pain, but he had no intention of lying in this bed tonight.

The nurse frowned at him. "Is someone coming to get you? You certainly can't drive yourself."

"Yes, ma'am. I've got a ride." He patted his hair down with his hand. "Do I look presentable for my date?"

"You're a rascal," the nurse said, smiling slightly. "You've got to go out in a wheelchair, but I can't release you. The doctor will be in to talk to you."

As if on cue, a tall man walked into the hospital room. "Mr. Hart, I presume?" he said, looking at the nurse instead of Cody.

"Yes, doctor, this is Mr. Hart. He refuses to be admitted," she said, glancing nervously at Cody.

"Hi, Doc. Don't blame her. She's done everything she can to get me back in bed," Cody said, looking at the blushing nurse. "Seriously, I'm not staying here. This isn't a prison, is it?"

The doctor frowned. "No, Mr. Hart, but you'll need

to sign some papers to release the hospital from responsibility since you're leaving prematurely … and against our advice." He examined Cody's wound. "You're lucky. Nothing vital was hit, so you should recover completely. But give it some time, okay?"

"Got it," Cody said.

The doctor then said to the nurse. "I'll bring him a shirt so he can visit his friend before he leaves. She's been asking about him."

Lena and Ayita were in the emergency area when the nurse took Cody to them. The nurse partially pushed aside the curtain surrounding the gurney. "Hi, there, beautiful," the nurse said to Ayita. "Someone wants to see you. Are you okay with that?"

Ayita nodded.

The nurse asked Lena's permission also. "It's Mr. Hart. Can he visit briefly?"

"Cody?" Lena asked. "Yes, of course. Is he alright?"

The nurse pushed the curtain aside further. "He's right out here in the hallway. I'll go get him." She walked out of the room and then wheeled Cody in, stopping close to the gurney.

"Thanks for everything," Cody said to the nurse. "Tell the doc I'll get his shirt back to him."

"I'm sure he'd want you to keep it," she said smiling. "Get well soon, Mr. Hart." As she turned to leave, she added. "Just a brief visit. Understand?" She looked at Cody, then Lena, both of whom nodded in agreement.

Cody wheeled himself closer to the foot of Ayita's bed. "So you're the young lady we've all been looking for."

Ayita smiled and shrugged. "I wasn't lost. Abe told me to stay inside and wait for Maker."

"You're a brave girl," Cody said."

"I wasn't scared most of the time." She lowered her head slightly. "But sometimes I was." Looking at Cody's bandaged chest and shoulder, she asked, "Did you get hurt?"

Cody smiled. "Yeah, but I'm getting well now." He turned to Lena. "Is she being admitted?"

Lena smiled at Ayita. "No, they said she's free to go. She's already been released, but we wanted to see you first." She leaned in slightly and said to Cody in a low voice. "She really doesn't understand what happened. The doctor said that's probably a good thing."

A sharp pain shot through Cody's shoulder, and he winced involuntarily as he slumped slightly.

"Are you okay?" Lena asked. "You need to rest."

Cody straightened himself in the wheelchair. "I'm fine. But you and Ayita need to ride back with me and Eddie. He'll be here soon to pick me up."

"Actually, we're spending the night in Asheville, at a hotel, courtesy of Ayita's Aunt Kat." She paused and then added, "If you feel like it, call me when you get back to the cabin. I feel bad I won't be there to help you."

"I will, but I'll be fine. It's not like the first time I've ever been shot."

"Does it hurt to get shot?" Ayita asked.

Cody smiled. "Yeah, it really does. But I'll be fine."

"I'll ask the ravens to watch over you," Ayita said.

CHAPTER SIXTY-FIVE

Cody awoke to a noise. What was it? Again, that noise. He managed to open his eyes, and the sunlight through the window was unbearable. Was it morning? No, the sun was in the West, so it must be afternoon. For just a moment, he thought he was at home in New Mexico, with Nora.

"Cody, it's me, Lena. Are you decent? Can I come in?"

"Wait a sec," Cody called out. He looked down and realized he still had his jeans on. Eddie had insisted on taking him home with him, but Cody just needed the time alone. "I'm mostly decent."

Lena opened the door. "You left the door unlocked last night." She held up her hand. "Don't get up." She sat in the upholstered chair and rubbed its threadbare arm. "My grandmother gave me this chair. It needs to be redone. I'll take care of it soon."

"The memories are more important than the chair." Cody leaned back on the pillow.

Lena wiped tears from her face with the back of her hand. "I was so worried about you." She managed to laugh and cry simultaneously. "But I should have known you're too hardheaded and too stubborn to die."

"Yeah, I've been accused of that a few times." He turned his head to look at her. "But thanks for caring." He propped himself up in bed and pulled the cover over his bare chest. "On the way here, Eddie told me about finding Maker's body. Have you told Ayita?"

Lena shook her head. "I left that to Kat to handle. She picked up Ayita this morning at the hotel, and Eddie had an agent bring me back here." Lena looked down and sighed. "Kat is Ayita's temporary guardian now." Lena looked away and pulled a tissue from her jeans pocket. "I can't believe all this has happened. Abe's dead, Maker's dead."

"I guess I brought bad luck to Raven's Rest, huh?" Cody said.

"No, I mean, well. You had to come here, didn't you?"

"Do you know about the bracelet they found in the mine?" he asked Lena. "Eddie told me about it while we were driving back here.

She shook her head, so he told her what he knew, which wasn't much. "I'm sure it belonged to Nora, but I don't know what to make of it," he said.

"What will you do now?"

Cody shrugged. "What can I do that I haven't already done? The only two people who *may* know anything about Nora, if there is anything to know, are gone. Maybe there's a rational explanation for why her bracelet was in the mine. Maybe she …"

Lena looked at him, tears spilling down her cheeks.

"What will happen to Ayita now?" Cody asked, changing the subject.

"I'm not sure. Kat and Ayita really don't know each other." Lena smiled slightly, as she dabbed at her eyes with a tissue. "But they seem to hit it off pretty good."

"It would be a shame to take Ayita away from here. She seems to love that field and those ravens."

Lena nodded. "I agree. But it's not up to us to decide." She glanced away, looking toward the sunlight streaming through the window. "What will you do now?"

"Honestly, I'm not sure. I have a job waiting for me in New Mexico. If I want it, that is. And I don't know what I can do here. I'll have to earn a paycheck at some point."

Lena fingered the hem at the tail of her shirt. "I hope you can stay. I mean, I've gotten used to having you here." She shrugged. "Besides, you haven't helped me fix this place up yet. That was our deal, right?"

"You're a tough landlady, you know that?" Cody said. "I need to heal. And to think. I'm still a bit out of it, so making major life decisions at this moment is not a good idea." He smiled. "Whatever I decide, I'll help you before I go. Deal?"

Lena stood, answering softly. "Deal. I'm going to let you sleep, but I'll bring you some soup for lunch if you're up to eating. You've missed a few meals, you know."

As she opened the door, Cody said, "Thanks for being a good friend, Lena. I really appreciate all you've done."

Cody remembered little of the rest of the day. The pain pills were doing what they were supposed to do, so he slept. But when he woke up later that evening, his head ached, not to mention his bandaged shoulder.

He managed to get out of bed and then saw a note on the table. It was from Lena, saying she had put his soup in the refrigerator and that she would lock the door on the way out. Cody smiled to himself. Lena was one of the good ones.

Stumbling to the bathroom, he steadied himself against the door frame. No more pills, he decided. He'd rather have pain than to feel like this, so out of control. The thought of food wasn't very appealing right now, so he'd save the soup for later.

As he slowly made his way back to sit on the bed, he heard a knock on the door. When he unlocked the door and opened it slightly, Eddie was standing there grinning. "Hey, buddy. Want some company?" Eddie pushed the door open and walked past Cody without waiting for an answer. "Too bad, I'm coming in anyway."

Cody smiled. "I'd expect nothing less." He pointed to the bed. "I need to sit down. I'm not too steady on my feel just yet." When Eddie took a step forward to help him, Cody waved him off. "I'm fine. Really," he said as he half sat, half fell onto the bed.

Eddie sat down across from Cody. "I just wanted to check on you. Other than being on a cheap drunk from pain pills, how are you feeling?"

Cody shrugged. "Honestly, I'm not sure. Physically, I'll heal. But I'm … I don't know what to do from here. Any news on Skip?"

Eddie shook his head. "No, buddy, but we're still looking. We won't stop until we find him." He paused briefly. "But we don't know if he'll have any information on Nora. The bracelet doesn't guarantee she was here."

"My gut tells me she was here. But not now. That's just a feeling, nothing to base it on."

"I know, man, it's not a good situation, no matter what." Eddie slapped his palms on his thighs. "So, what's next? You staying, going home, what?"

"Why is everybody asking me that today?" Cody asked, recalling his conversation with Lena. "Was I that much trouble that you're all trying to get rid of me?"

Eddie laughed. "You are a bit of a pain in the ass, for sure." His expression then became more serious. "But actually, I hope you'll consider staying."

"And do what?" Cody asked. "Lena wants me to help her fix up the cabin a bit, and I will, but that's in exchange for rent. I can't—"

"Would you be quiet for a minute," Eddie said. "I'm trying to offer to you a solution. If New Mexico is willing to let you transfer here on a temporary assignment with the SBI, we could sure use your skills. We get missing hikers and campers, fugitives hiding out, poachers—you know, the same kind of cases you handled back home. NC Forestry has a full plate, just like everyone else, so they can't help us too much. And our agents aren't nearly as skilled as you are in this kind of environment." He spread his arms out, palms up. "So, whaddaya say?"

Cody leaned back against the headboard and closed his eyes. "As I told Lena, this is not the day to make those kinds of decisions." He turned to look at Eddie.

Eddie leaned forward. "Look, I get it. If and when you're ready, I think we can get your superiors to loan you to the Forestry Service here, you know, on special assignment to assist the SBI. But we'd have to work all that out. If you're interested, that is." Eddie stood. "But we can talk later. Anything you need before I go?"

Yes, I need answers. I need Nora back. "No, I'm good. Thanks."

CHAPTER SIXTY-SIX

For the next few days, Cody focused on rest and recovery. Lena was like a mother hen, bringing him food, offering to clean the cabin, or to sit with him if he was lonely.

Lena said Eddie had checked on Cody several times but had not stopped by. Maybe Eddie had changed his mind about the job offer. Cody wasn't sure he wanted to accept it anyway. Then again, what was there for him in New Mexico if he went back there? He'd immerse himself into his old work to occupy his mind, but then he'd have to go home alone, to an empty house. Maybe it was time for him to start building a life without Nora. As painful as that realization was, the thought of living in grief and uncertainty for the rest of his life was even more frightening.

It was nearly lunchtime, so perhaps he'd go to the dining room to eat, instead of staying in the cabin, which was getting increasingly smaller each day. Moving slowly, Cody put on fresh clothes and ran his hand through his dark hair. He needed a haircut.

When he walked into the dining area, he was shocked to see Kat and Ayita sitting at a table. "Well, my goodness," he said to Ayita, "it's so good to see you again." Cody looked across the table at Kat. "And you too."

"We're going to dance with the ravens," Ayita said. "Will you come with us?"

Cody smiled. "I'd love to, but maybe some other time.

I'm still a bit wobbly."

"What's wobbly?" Ayita asked.

Kat laughed at Ayita. "It means, young lady, that he's still healing from being … " She stopped, as if unsure whether saying "shot" would be too disturbing. "He just needs to rest."

"But I can come watch you after I grab some lunch," Cody said. "How about that?"

Ayita enthusiastically nodded her head in agreement and then picked up another chicken nugget. Kat reached out and put her hand on Cody's arm. "We'll talk later."

After finishing his lunch, Cody slowly walked to the field. Lena had offered to drive him, but he needed to move. After nearly two weeks of rest and recuperation, Cody had much of his strength back, but his left hand still had some tingling in it. The doctor said it was possibly nerve damage, but after Cody had refused to agree to drive to Asheville for physical therapy, they gave Cody a series of exercises to do at home.

Walking was helpful, not just for Cody's body, but also for his soul. For the first time since coming to Raven's Rest, he allowed himself to appreciate its beauty. He wasn't a religious man, but he believed in the spirits his ancestors had revered. Standing at the edge of Ayita's field, with her beloved ravens overhead, Cody looked upward to the mountain peaks.

He was beginning to accept he might not ever know

what happened to Nora. He couldn't explain this gut feeling to Lena or Eddie, but he *knew* somehow that she had been here, in or near this area. After pushing the unthinkable out of his mind for more than a year, Cody now tried to accept that perhaps Nora was in some faraway country. Perhaps an older man considered Nora, in her mid-thirties, to be the perfect age for his wife and had purchased her online through Skip, Abe, or others like them who profited from others' sorrow.

Or perhaps she was buried, somewhere here in the mountains, where she had wanted to visit again. He may never know.

Some days, the hopelessness overcame him. On other days, he vowed to make something of his life instead of spending every waking moment thinking about Nora.

When Ayita saw Cody, she ran over to him. "Watch me dance with Nali."

Cody smiled. "Who is Nali? One of your ravens?"

Ayita frowned. "No, Nali is in heaven, but when I dance, she comes back to see me."

"Ah, I see," Cody said, although he wasn't sure what she meant.

Ayita ran across the field and began twirling and chanting something Cody couldn't make out. Apparently, she had created her own language that only she and the ravens understood. Suddenly, a half dozen ravens began circling the field, calling out to her. He walked over to where Kat was standing, watching Ayita.

"Who or what is Nali?" Cody asked.

"As far as Ayita knows, Maker was her grandmother, her only family. Cherokee often call their grandmothers

Nali."

Cody nodded. "She loves this place, doesn't she," he said.

Although Kat was smiling, the sadness in her expression was undeniable. "Yes, she does." She waved at Ayita. "I'm not sure what to do. I've never had maternal instincts, and even if I asked Ayita to come to Columbia to live with me, she would be unhappy there." Kat shook her head. "I just don't know what to do."

"Perhaps you could move here, or to Asheville," Cody said.

"My work, my life, are not here. The mountains are beautiful, but you have to adapt to this life." She looked at Cody, her face furrowed with worry. "As lovely as the mountains are, they're not for me."

Cody kicked at a loose rock. "This may seem far-fetched, but what about Lena?"

Kat turned to face Cody. "Lena? What do you mean? Adoption?"

"Well, maybe. I'm not sure. But Lena has a mothering instinct, and she loves Ayita. They played together before … before all this happened. I sometimes got the impression Ayita was closer to Lena than Maker. All I'm saying is it's worth a conversation. Lena may say 'no thanks,' but at least you'll have tried."

Ayita's voice floated through the air as she danced and sang. "You can't ask her to leave all this," Cody said to Kat. "It's where she belongs."

Kat nodded. "Yes, but Ayita is too young to make these kinds of decisions. I've told her when she's older, this land is hers, and she can do what she wants with it." Kat smiled. "She wants to have a raven sanctuary and a place for children to dance with them."

"Not surprising," Cody said, suddenly exhausted. "I'm going back to the cabin. Tell Ayita I said goodbye."

Kat nodded, and then as Cody was leaving, she called out to him, "This is where you belong too."

CHAPTER SIXTY-SEVEN

For the first time in weeks, Cody was able to move his arm without pain and his strength was returning. The weather had turned cold, and he was enjoying being outdoors and hiking again.

After several more conversations with Eddie, Cody turned down the SBI's offer. Eddie pressed him to reconsider, but Cody was resolute in his decision, even if he had no idea where to go or what to do next.

During one of their conversations, Eddie told Cody that several days ago they had found Skip's Jeep Wrangler down the side of a mountain, likely pushed over the side rather than an accident. A thorough search had not turned up Skip's body or anything else of interest. The trail was cold, and there was some speculation that Skip had managed to get out of the country. Perhaps one of Skip's overseas clients had given him safe haven.

The SBI had gone through everything in Skip's real estate office: laptop, iPad, and paper files. But they found nothing to help locate Skip—nor any trace of Nora.

Cody would soon be released by the doctor and free to leave. But to go where? Technically, he was still on leave from the New Mexico Forestry Service. But until he decided his next step, he had busied himself helping Lena at the store and doing light repairs on the cabin. He also tried to focus on rediscovering who he was—the man he was without Nora. She was no longer a part of his life. Not by choice, but by a cruel twist of fate.

Sam, Lena's cousin in Columbia, had called a few times and hinted she might visit. But Cody was careful not to encourage her. He wasn't ready for a relationship with her—or anyone else. Not yet.

During these last weeks of his recovery, he also helped Lena work out a routine that allowed her to maintain the general store and diner—and to get used to her new role caring for Ayita. While Kat had legal custody, she and Lena had agreed to share responsibility for raising Ayita. However, the child whose name fittingly meant "first to dance" spent most of her time in Raven's Rest, to no one's surprise.

And Lena, at last, had someone to mother. Cody had never learned any more about her past than what Sonny had told him. He hoped she would open up to him one day about her own life, her own sorrow.

For now, Cody was a babysitter and handyman, while providing whatever support Lena needed as she settled into life with Ayita.

Standing in Ayita's field one day, Cody made a quiet vow to allow himself to be happy again—not someday, but now, in the small ways that mattered. Sorrow would never leave him completely, but neither would hope. And for now, that was enough.

∞

Author's Note

As my loyal readers know, each of my books is inspired by an actual crime or event. I don't write about these events explicitly; rather, I focus on the underlying themes, with the real-life victims serving as my muses. I remind myself that I'm writing for *them* – the real victims. Asha Degree was my muse for *One for Sorrow.*

In 2000, nine-year-old Asha Degree vanished from her home in Shelby, North Carolina, sparking one of the most haunting missing child cases in recent memory. Despite early sightings of her walking alone in the dark and the later discovery of her backpack miles away, her disappearance has remained unsolved for over two decades. Recent developments—including DNA evidence and search warrants—have pointed to possible suspects and a vehicle linked to the case, but Asha's remains have never been found, and no arrests have been made.

Asha's case reminds us that behind every headline is a life, a family, and a story that deserves to be told.

As for this fictional story about Cody, my husband and I first discussed it back in 2007—nine years before my first mystery novel was published. We even sketched a floor plan for the general store featured in the book. But as often happens, life got in the way, and I put Cody's story aside.

In 2016, I published *Murder in Madden,* the first Enid Blackwell novel. If you've followed the series, you know that there are seven books in that series. However, when I decided to start a new series and began imagining a fictional story to capture the theme of Asha Degree's disappearance, I ran across our notes about Cody from decades ago. That's how *One for Sorrow* came into being.

The Cody Hart Series will include three stories. If you've finished this book, you know questions remain—by design, of course. So stay tuned for books two and three—all questions will be answered.

As for the Ravens Rest setting, I've been fascinated by the Blue Ridge Mountains all my life. There's something mysterious and spiritual about this area. Of course, the town of Ravens Rest is a figment of my imagination.

And ravens have long fascinated me. Many years ago, I tracked down a somewhat rare copy of *Ravens and Black Rain: The Story of Highland Second Sight,* by Elizabeth Sutherland. That was the beginning of my fascination with these brilliant, mysterious, often maligned birds.

Thank you for continuing to support my work. Words cannot express my gratitude for the loyalty and appreciation you, my readers, have shown me. Writing a book is hard work, but it's also a labor of love—love of words, storytelling, and readers like you.

Acknowledgments

Of all the words I write, these few pages are the most meaningful. Without the support of those around me, none of this would be possible.

First and foremost, I want to thank my wonderful spouse, William Earl Craig. He calls himself my "roadie," as he's responsible for maintaining our book inventory for in-person events, packing the truck for festivals, and helping me set up and break down each event. Yet he's so much more: my rock, my foundation, my chief cheerleader. He supports me in countless ways that allow me to do what I do, year after year.

Just as importantly, he was the inspiration for Cody's personal character traits: strong but sensitive—and a loving husband.

I also want to thank Irene Stern, "The Novel Mechanic," my friend, developmental editor, and supporter. She has contributed to my success in many ways over the years.

During the early stages of developing Cody's character, I got stuck. Over lunch with my friend A.C. Blake—an author, poet, illustrator, and former professor—she suggested Cody could be a forestry service investigator. Bingo! That was exactly the solution I needed.

Finally, my heartfelt thanks to all the friends, fellow writers, and readers who've joined me on this incredible journey over the past decade.

Raegan

ABOUT THE AUTHOR

Choosing our own name is a privilege few of us have—except perhaps, fiction writers. In this domain, I am known as Raegan Teller, a name I've chosen with care and purpose.

Raegan means "spiritual strength," and the surname Teller, synonymous with "storyteller" in English, reflects my passion for weaving narratives that captivate and intrigue.

Behind the pen name, I am Wanda Craig, whose diverse career spans business writing, copy editing, marketing, executive coaching, corporate training, and insurance management. My journey also includes a unique stint selling burial vaults during my school years—a fitting precursor to my fascination with mystery writing.

My affinity for mystery and suspense novels runs deep, influenced by every author whose work I've had the pleasure of reading. My literary tastes are eclectic—my favorite author often being whoever wrote the last compelling book I've devoured. However, the authors I gravitate toward are those whose narratives frequently explore family dynamics and the emotional depth of their characters, with the elements of murder and crime serving to enhance their personal journeys and the turmoil faced.

As Raegan Teller, I strive to join the ranks of such storytellers—those who delve into human complexities and relationships, weaving mysteries that keep readers eagerly turning pages. I hope you find that my stories resonate with you, offering both intrigue and a glimpse into the intricacies of the human heart.

PLEASE…

A humble request from the author

Thank you for taking the time to read my book. The world needs more readers like you.

I hope you enjoyed *One for Sorrow*. If so, please do me a big favor and leave a review on Amazon and/or Goodreads. Reviews encourage readers to discover authors they might otherwise overlook.

Thank you so much for your support!

Leave your review here:
Amazon: www.Amazon.com
Goodreads: **www.Goodreads.com**

I'd love to hear your thoughts! Reach out anytime through my website: www.RaeganTeller.com/contact

Printed in Dunstable, United Kingdom

78435881R00170